RICHARD CARLILE

Carlile Originals

WWW.CARLILE.MEDIA

A DIVISION OF CREADYNE DEVELOPMENTS LLC, MINDEN, NV

This edition is dedicated with gratitude to those readers who, seeing something of interest in this little book and recommending it to others, have by word of mouth given it the breath which kept it alive and so have helped bring about its re-issue after almost half a century.

Foreword

From *Girl Gangs, Biker Boys, and Real Cool Cats: Pulp Fiction and Youth Culture, 1950 to 1980*

A future world dominated by vast discrepancies in wealth and power, and shaped by sex, drugs and rock and roll, with lashings of violence, riots and revolution, not to mention transvestites and deviant sex. It's a hell of a ride in Richard Carlile's *Drummer*. There's barely a pulp fiction button left unpressed.

And yet, this is no straightforward exploitation novel of the kind churned out by Carlile's contemporaries over at the New English Library. You notice the difference from the outset: no one else writing paperback originals in Britain in the early 1970s was likely to use the word 'mnesic' in their opening paragraph.

Carlile had left St. Andrew's University in 1969, where he had studied English literature and philosophy. Disillusioned with literary fiction, and feeling that 'things had turned bad' with the counter-culture, he threw himself into producing a lurid vision of the future that would be deliberately unliterary. Written at speed, and published exactly as written with no editorial input, *Drummer* was one of the first works to articulate the comedown from the cultural high of the 1960s.

The story is of Ariston, an erstwhile drummer eking out an existence on the rubbish dumps of 'a city without a name', who gets recruited into Satiety Incorporated, a small-time band just about to break big. When they do, it's to the accompaniment of a 'civic war' that almost brings society to its knees. Ariston, however, is removed from these wider concerns. During his starving, scavenging days, he had resorted to eating the liquefying pulp of the city's garbage, an unidentifiable substance somewhere between Viagra and Larry Cohen's The Stuff, that keeps him just about alive and gives him enormous sexual staying power. Consequently he finds himself adopted as a lover by the sex-starved wife of a movie producer. And then the story starts to go weird, as Ariston descends into a world of horror, murder, sadism and biker gangs...

Actually the narrative pretty much defies rational analysis. This is an impressionistic collage of scenes and images that makes as much sense as a nightmare, and has the same lingering, haunting power.

The closest parallel is probably David Bowie's *Diamond Dogs* album from 1974, another fragmentary dystopia that documents the decline of the progressive dream. And the proto-glam of *Drummer* also prefigures the transgender fixation of glitter rock, with its depiction of the Doll People, a youth tribe comprised of boys brought up as girls so they can be sold into marriage to wealthy, decadent pederasts. When those relationships inevitably collapse, the Doll People drift into the streets, a collection of 'subtly merging heteroclites' whose erratic, unpredictable behaviour symbolises the instability of a society that is careering out of control.

But despite its post-Altamont origins, *Drummer* isn't fixed in time, largely because Carlile had the good sense not to attempt any description of the music played by Satiety Incorporated. I first read it in the late 1970s, when punk was at its peak, and it made perfect sense then in the context of the Sex Pistols and of Derek Jarman's film *Jubilee*. It still does in a world of transglobal corporations and growing economic inequality.

Alwyn W. Turner

Our future hurries to become our past. Our enemy death,
first distant as a star, its stellar farness light-fast diminishes
until it stands close by or sits, more true friend now
than foe, patient beside the bed where life finishes.

Floating on the River of Forever

IT WAS a city without a name, the capital of a country without borders or limits, a sweating, garish, seemingly endless conurbation synthesized out of an incestuous intermingling of the goodtime districts and fun ghettos of a badtime and unfunny world, so that the streets of what might have been misnamed its heart consisted almost entirely of amusement arcades, cinemas, nightclubs, stripclubs, dance halls, bars, casinos, restaurants, snack bars, hotels, cafés. ... Different parts of the city, even different parts of the same street, reminded you in a vague way of diverse places; yet the mnesic effect depended as much on what you had been as on where you had been. Thus it was truly a cosmopolis.

For Ariston it was confusing. He had grown up among the city's noise and glare, and the streets with their gabble of signs and advertisements, their smells of hot dogs and engine fumes and their way of seeming like somewhere else, somewhere he could never quite remember, were familiar to him. He could find his way about, but he knew the city only by rote. Familiarity had quieted the fear and panic he had endured as a child, but the confusion remained, and tonight, maybe because he was so hungry and tired, the confusion was worse than ever.

No matter how the city seemed to twist and distort itself, to play tricks on him, to lay snares, he remained calm. He knew he would survive. He always had, always would. And sometimes he had done more than merely survive – had lived in luxury. Once there had been plenty of food, plenty of drink, plenty of everything, and he had lived in one of the high-priced hotels that overlooked the beach. That was when he had worked with Pete.

Now, without Pete, he wasn't doing so well. No balconied hotel suite now, just a shack out on the rubbish dump. He had made it himself, though, and was proud of it. For the most part it was built around the remains of a huge wooden packing-case. After scouring the junk heaps for any usable length of clapboard and tin sheeting, he had hammered together quite a cozy little home for himself. As for living among rubbish, that wasn't so bad once he had grown used to it, and he had come to like the smell of the dump, the rich, moldering, autumnal smell that was like the taste of fruit cake. Big brown rats swarmed in the refuse but he was on friendly terms with them, and it was only occasionally that the wind switched from its usual direction and dragged the acrid smoke from the distant, ever-smoldering ash-pits over towards the shack. He had gradually become accustomed to everything, accepted everything, even that when he had eaten nothing for five, six days and just had to have something – anything – to appease the gnawing in his stomach, he should make use of the piles of decomposing restaurant leftovers. ... Even that he had got used to.

Where the Reeperbahn ran into the Plaza de Garibaldi was the Golden Spittoon, a bar and dance club. Ariston had been standing outside the place for about three hours now. He was sure that eventually he would see a familiar face there, and then he would maybe be able to cadge the price of a bite to eat. A sandwich and a cola were all he needed to keep him going for another day. For almost three hours he had been standing there on the sidewalk, and every now and then his eyes shifted from the faces of the passers-by and he glanced across the neon-lit square to a broad avenue that led down to the promenade and the sea. It was a time poised between late afternoon and the beginning of evening. The sun hung two-thirds down the sky, an orange sun that peered myopically through a tenuous but clinging miasma of fog and mist. Everything at a distance of more than thirty yards was subdued, anonymous, etherealized. The horizon was lost and perspective dissolved. The tide was in, and the darkening sea lay sluggish and woebegone. The sun's reflection was a narrow, gently shimmering path, and it was only by following this pathway back across the water to where it stopped that the eye could make an estimate of where the dark blue-gray sea ended and the dark gray-blue sky began. Opposing the strengthening darkness, the city's neon lamps and lights flickered and flared, stared and glared, twinkling, winking, and the animated illuminations – a peacock spreading its tail-feathers, a man raising and draining a tankard – jerked unconvincingly, while far away the gigantic Ferris wheel rotated dreamily.

Ariston turned his eyes back to the faces.

The faces. The corrupt, ugly, meaningless faces eager for fun. Ugly, everyone he saw was ugly. Except the doll people of course. Slim and perfect, dressed in weird but becoming fashions, they floated past him, their long-lashed doe eyes blinking dopily. They glanced neither to left nor right, seemed to see no-one and nothing. You never knew where you were with them. You could never be sure what they had in mind to do next. Their emotions were completely unstable, completely unpredictable. For no clear reason they would swing from their usual sluggish languor to screaming hysteria, and the media were always full of stories about them and their crazy ideas, their religious fads, their phases of destructiveness. Without warning cohorts of them were liable to stampede through the streets laughingly tossing home-made explosives here and there. Their sublime indifference to the effects on others of their petrol- and paraffin-bombs was equaled by the fatalistic passivity of their acceptance of the frenzy of punishment the police dealt out in return: as truncheons smashed their skulls they made esoteric and holy signs, as bullets shattered their chests and their bright life-blood spurted on to the roadway they smiled benignly.

It was quite dark now. The lights and illuminations, never turned off even at noon, came into their own, blossoming harshly, probing Ariston's weary eyes. The noise too seemed to have increased. His head throbbed, but still he stood there and watched the crowds, searching for a face he knew, someone who would help him. A hot dog and a cola. ...

It grew cold. He shivered. His eyes, his legs, ached. A face. ... Someone must come. ...

Suddenly some motorbike creeps, a gang of about thirty, came roaring out of a side street, their engines machine-gunning the night into immediate submission. Passers-by froze in their tracks or scurried for what shelter they could find. For a while the creeps amused themselves by playing cowboys, by racing along the sidewalks and chasing doll people into the middle of the square, crowding them there into a denser and denser mass by burning round them in ever-decreasing circles. Some cops, hating both groups equally and not caring if any of them got hurt, not considering the fracas any of their business as long as no property was damaged or okay citizen hurt, lounged in a nearby patrol car and watched.

The doll people had been expertly herded into a tight cluster. In spite of the deafening noise and the dangerous exhibitionistic antics of the motorbike creeps, they remained quiescent. Careening machines shot around them with only inches to spare: the riders drove furiously straight at them, braking and turning only at the last moment; still the doll people were serene. It lasted about five minutes, then at some signal the spinning circumference of black leather and gleaming metal neatly peeled itself off into a straight line and rocketed away, the gang vanishing as mysteriously as they had appeared, going fast, going nowhere. De-corralled, the doll people dispersed dreamily, though some stayed in the middle of the square chatting in bevies of four or five or just chewing gum and staring vacantly.

With a thrust of his shoulders Ariston pushed himself away from the glass wall of the Golden Spittoon. It was a long walk back to the dump.

An hour or so later he was there, stumbling and falling repeatedly as he made his unlit way across the piles of refuse towards his shack. He was tired, so very tired, but hunger tormented him. Before he slept he had to have something, anything. In the darkness he staggered around, then dropped to his knees. His hands felt in front of him. This was the right place, the pile he had eaten from last time. Without hesitation he pushed his arm wrist-deep into the decomposing mush and pulled out a fistful of the porridgy stuff. He lowered his face to his cupped palm, his lips parting, pushing out and curling back to form a kind of sucker as his mouth sought its nourishment.

A SIDE street in a quiet area. A dead area. Some of the lamps were broken and the long corridor of concrete and brick was in semi-darkness. Pete stood at the mouth of an alleyway and glanced left and right. No-one. He sank back into the blackness.

Darkness and silence held hands here in the alley, but their clasping fingers were harshly torn apart a moment later as Pete stepped blindly into a covey of empty beer bottles, sending them clattering and scattering ringingly away from him. Fuck it. Fuck the bloody things. He froze, listening. From somewhere came the noise of a party and from a brightly lit open window nearby the voices of a man and woman hoarsely quarrelling. That was all. No-one had heard. No-one would be interested, anyway. Everybody minded his own business. He could have practiced his drums here and no-one would have bothered. But he was jumpy. His hands were shaking. Nerves. Keep your head, Pete boy, and get on with the job. It's easy, this one, nothing to them, these ancient pharmacies run by doddering pharmacists who never retire. A walk-in. ...

A few more moments just to make sure everything was all right, to calm down a little more, then he moved on, picking his way as though in a minefield.

He reached the fence, clambered up and dropped down the other side. This was the backyard of the pharmacy – should be, that is, if there hadn't been some stupid mistake, like the time he was stoned and spent half the night cutting through a ceiling only to find himself in a health food store. Now he was at the window, taping over one of the panes. A smart controlled blow with the side of his gloved fist on the tape, and then he quickly peeled off the broad fragment-stuck strip.

Carefully he waggled free an awkward shard from the frame, slipped his hand through and unscrewed the catch. The window slid up and in a jiffy he was inside the back room of the pharmacy.

He was growing more excited. Couldn't help himself. Store room equaled drugs. He quivered in tight spasms. The beam of his torch flitted shakily around the room, over packing-cases, shelves, an old rolltop desk, then settled on a black cabinet. He went up to it, praying the pharmacist hadn't had the wit to update the lock. ... No, it was a museum piece. Not even very strong, by the look of it – might be able just to force it. He poised the torch on a shelf so that he got the benefit of its light, took a slim jimmy from his pocket, slipped it in beside the lock, levered – immediately, like a blow on the head, the alarm screamed hysterically in his ears. The jimmy fell from his fingers, thumped onto the floorboards. He bent, groped for it, found it, straightened, jammed it in again and straining, baring his teeth, levered with all his strength. The alarm bell rang on, on, on. It was unbelievably loud – seemed to be inside his head. Sweat beaded his forehead. He made a final effort, throwing his full weight onto the jimmy. The lock snapped, the door sprang open. Seizing the torch, he shone it over the neat rows of labeled bottles and packets. He saw some methedrine, grabbed it, stuffed it into his pockets. There was drinamyl too; he rammed pack after pack into one pocket after another until they would take no more. All the time the fucking bell yelling its stupid head off. Somehow he expected it to run down like an alarm clock. Loaded, he whirled round and ran across the store room and through to the front of the pharmacy – no time for the back way now – picked up a small display case from the counter and hurled it at the door. Its long central glass panel exploded and, tripping, almost falling over the display case, Pete stumbled out onto the sidewalk.

The alarm bell had cracked the silence of the deserted street, now the crash of glass shattered it. At an apartment window up there a dark silhouette appeared, stood watching. Over at that one another black cut-out of a human figure popped into place. Between the warring couple hostilities had paused. The man's attention diverted, he swiveled his scowling face towards the window, as though ready for a fresh, perhaps more interesting threat from elsewhere.

– Wha' the ... ?

Stepping to the window, he leaned out on his thick hairy forearms. One apish arm rose, gesturing to his mate behind him, not threatening her now but, like the comradely tone of his voice, summoning her to share this.

—Hey, c'mere, May, som'dy jus' done the pharmacy again – wow, look at that boy go!

Feet pounding the sidewalk, Pete raced for the corner. He cut across a vacant lot, ran on down a short alley, staggered out. There, waiting at the curb, was his car. Cursing himself for parking so far away, he tore open the door, threw himself in, slammed the door shut. As he straightened up he suddenly, to his surprise, felt sickish, weak, unfocused, felt his strength going, going quite quickly, draining out of him as though down some opened plughole. His hands gripped the steering wheel, his head dipped, eyes closed. Immediately he opened his eyes. He had to get out of here *now*. Forcing himself to concentrate, he reached for the keys in the ignition. It was only as his fingers fumbled with them that he noticed the blood. His sleeve was soaked with it, it was dripping from the cuff, and only then, staring at the dripping blood, did he become aware of the pain, a throbbing, in his neck. He touched the place, took his hand away covered with blood. He swore, as though exasperated by some nuisance, some further inconvenience, leaned forward and twisted the key in the ignition.

The car jerked away from the curb, shot away down the street. Thirty yards on, just before the corner, Pete blacked out from loss of blood and the car, instead of turning either left or right, rocketed straight across the junction and hurled itself suicidally against the waiting wall opposite.

When the explosive noise of the crash died away the shop alarm bell could be heard ringing on and on. That was all.

It was a quiet area. A dead area.

As IN one of its cinematic reproductions of the Wild West, the city enjoyed perfect weather. The sun there was a simple, dependable, extrovert sort of fellow who could be relied on to leap cheerfully out of bed each dawn and blaze away unremittingly with his solar six-shooters till reloading time, then to ride off down the ol' sunset trail and disappear beyond a filmic panorama of dust clouds. Thus it had been another beautiful day – a lucky one too for Ariston, for had he not found not one, not two, but three coins on the beach where some bather had piled his clothes carelessly? He had. Now it was evening again, and Ariston sat at a table in the Golden Spittoon. Having taken his fill of hot dogs, he was savoring a beer, enjoying being on the inside of the bar looking out. He waved cheerily to a few people he didn't know, laughed foolishly, sipped his drink.

   –You look as though you're enjoying yourself.

Ariston twisted round in his seat and looked up. He saw a young man of about his own age, tall, with abundant fair hair flowing down to the shoulders of a sharp three-piece suit, smiling down at him sardonically.

   –Hi, Malk, he greeted, half-rising. –Hey, you're looking good.

Malk put his hand on Ariston's shoulder, pressing him gently back down onto his seat.

   –Feelin' good, he murmured, sitting down and slipping out his cigarette case. –And you?

Ariston fumbled a reluctant, half-awake cigarette away from its sleeping companions.

   –Oh, I'm fine. Up and down. You know how it is.

—Uhuh.

Malk nodded solemnly. His lighter flared. He watched Ariston suck at the flame and his look flicked from the thin grimy face to the torn denim jacket, the filthy T-shirt showing underneath it. *Moujik*, he thought. But he'll do for tonight. Seems he'll have to.

—What're you drinking? Beer? C'mon, have a whisky.

He signaled to a waiter, gave his order.

While he waited for the drinks to arrive he tilted back in his chair and had a last look around in the hope of seeing an alternative. The drinks came. He eyed Ariston, sighed, lifted his glass to him.

—Well, here's to you.

Malk tossed back his drink and stared gloomily at the stage at the far end of the bar. A fat man had just waddled up to the mike and a crackling came over the speakers as he adjusted the stand. He cleared his throat, then words poured out.

—Good evening, ladies and gents. I'm certainly glad to be here at the Golden Spittoon tonight, because I'm getting paid. Ha-ha. No, seriously, as your compere I want to offer you a big welcome an' I can promise you some fine entertainers tonight – I can promise them but I can't produce them. Ha-ha. No, seriously, I'm worried about my hair – it's been coming out in large handfuls. I just wish I had smaller hands. ...

His worn-out patter poured out, hardly audible above the ambient noise, no-one, as he was depressingly aware, even trying to hear.

—What're you doing here, Malk? The group not playing tonight?

—Later. We're on at ten at the Flamingo. That's less than two hours from now and I don't have a drummer.

—What about Pete?

—Exactly. What about him? That's what I've been asking myself since he didn't turn up for practice today.

—What d'you think's happened?

—Dunno. I've been looking every damn where for him. You any idea where he might be?

—Me?

—Yes, you. You used to go around together, you two.

Ariston shook his head.

—Long time no see.

—It doesn't matter. I gave up hope of finding him hours ago. He'll re-appear, as is his wont, in his own sweet mystic time.

Malk jerked out the showy handkerchief that drooped from his breast pocket, wiped his fingers and pushed it back. He eyed Ariston condescendingly.

—You play drums as well as guitar, yeah?

—Pete taught me.

—Yep, I suppose that would be right. And you were drummer in some band too for a while – had a couple of lucky hits, right? What was it called again?

—The Candy Floss Machine.

—Yeah, I remember now. Your sound was crap. With lyrics to match. Hardly surprising you folded.

With a flick of his hand his dismissed the topic.

—Anyway, here's the offer. You play for us tonight and – if you're all right – every night till Pete turns up. It'll be worth your while, don't worry about that. So how about it?

Ariston crushed out his cigarette.

—Man, I haven't held sticks in months. Almost a year.

Malk waved the words aside.

—So what? It's like riding a bicycle; once you know how, you don't forget.

Ariston said nothing. An intent expression on his face, he was poking his fingers about in the ashtray. Malk scowled.

—We're not asking for anything fancy, he said impatiently. —Just a beat to back us up, that's all. You can manage that much, can't you? A monkey could do it.

He got up, taking hold of Ariston by the arm.

—C'mon. There's not much time.

Ariston jerked himself free. He sat staring stubbornly at the tabletop, began paddling his ash-stained fingers in some spilled beer. Malk stared down at him; he felt completely exasperated but something told him to curb his temper and tongue. After a pause he said quietly:

—Well, are you coming or aren't you?

Not looking at him, Ariston stood up.

The two left the bar and outside on the sidewalk Malk hailed a taxi. The ride lasted about ten minutes and ended in a neon-flashing, loud-mouthed street near the great skeletal Tower of Fun. Ariston followed in Malk's wake as he shoved through the crowd and led the way into a quietly festering alley. Two strips of straggling grass (in the yellow light it looked greasy and artificial, like the kind used in window displays) and a liberal sprinkling of beer cans decorated its sides. The walls were scrawled with gang slogans. A van bearing the legend *Satiety Incorporated* browsed peacefully near some steps where a small pack of twelve- or thirteen-year-old girls loitered. They showed a limited interest at the sight of Malk. One or two listlessly held out autograph books.

—Piss off, muttered Malk, shouldering past them and trotting down the steps.

He took out a key and unlocked the door, locking it again when they were both on the other side.

Ariston was in a large basement littered with musical instruments and sound equipment and crowded with boxes and junk. Three lean, long-haired young men, dressed in a way that was both stagy and shoddy, were sprawled about drinking beer, listening to music, smoking. Malk walked over and turned the music off.

—Still no Pete? he asked, his voice fatalistic.

—Nope, said one.

Another one, lounging in a broken-down armchair, slowly turned his head and gazed at Ariston.

—Who's this?

The third cackled:

—*What's* this, you mean!

—Shut it, snapped Malk. —He's our drummer for tonight.

—What's yer name, then?

—Ariston.

—Ariston! Ooo, a touch of class there, upon my word.

—Yeah, *Ariston*, where'd you pick up a name like that, eh?

—That's Toots, that's Bobs, that's Sonny, introduced Malk, pointing at each in turn. —Don't bother with them.

—Yeah, don't bother with us, echoed Toots.

—Welcome to Satiety Incorporated, said Sonny. —Have a beer.

Malk was busying himself with the equipment, setting it up.

—Get yourselves ready, he told them. —We're gonna have an hour's runthrough before we go on.

Toots groaned, Bobs slid down in the armchair till he had almost disappeared, Sonny unconcernedly punctured another can of beer and began to pour its contents down his throat.

—C'mon, said Malk, fixing some leads. —Move yourselves.

—Include me out, mumbled Bobs. —I'm weary. My fingers hath lost their magic. A palsy doth afflict me.

—A pox doth afflict you, that's more likely, said Toots. —Too much pussy, that's your trouble. No sense of moderation. You're cunt crazy, my man.

—I believe sublimation is unhealthy, that's all.

Malk turned round.

—You lot have two speeds – dead slow and stop. Now for the last time – move!

—Aw, why not forget about it tonight? asked Toots. —Phone and tell them we can't make it.

Malk ran at him.

—MOVE!

Toots jumped off the packing case he was using as a seat and cringed melodramatically away from the oncoming Malk.

—Don't hit me, boss! he pleaded. —I'll do anything you say, just don't hit me any more!

Toots and Bobs goofed around, scrambling over the junk and boxes, whooping and yelling, dodging Malk and hiding from him among the shadows that the single dusty bulb couldn't reach. Sonny sedately finished his beer, tossed the can over his shoulder and picked up his guitar. Ariston settled himself behind the drums, took up the sticks, gave a few preliminary taps, a roll or two, and started to play.

After a minute Sonny quit tuning his guitar. The other three emerged slowly from the shadows. All four stood quietly and listened.

—Not bad, Malk commented when Ariston had finished. —Not bad at all. If you play like that at the Flamingo, that'll be just fine.

They had a quick rehearsal of the songs they would use that night, packed their gear in the van, then left.

THAT NIGHT at the Flamingo the audience consisted largely of doll people. They went mad about the group, raved about it. The new drummer, he was too much, way-out. He turned them on, blew their minds. They loved him. He was beyond it all, he was – but excuse me, some background information on this class of citizen wouldn't be out of place here, so ...

A NOTE ON THE ORIGINS AND NATURE
OF THE DOLL PEOPLE

For a long time it had been the widespread practice in the city (I use as my main authority Professor Lazlo Stiel's monumental work *Male And Female Concubinage*) for a parent to act as arbiter with regard to the sexuality of his or her children, the degrees of masculinity and femininity in a child's character being determined by early social training and emotional conditioning aided to a greater or lesser extent by the administration of drugs. In many cases a parent, sometimes out of mere whim, sometimes for reasons outlined below, decided on a complete reversal of sex roles for a certain child (this decision often contradicting a previous, *prenatal* sex choice).

In instances where females were chosen for masculinization they were usually those who were physically unattractive or who displayed some emotional abnormality indicative of a potentially neurasthenic or neurotic personality. Being considered poor candidates for marriage, these girls were shaped to be able to fend for themselves. Thus the object of the remolding of a female child was generally to enable her to survive in a highly competitive and still in many ways male world. The processing, however, allowed considerable scope for re-adaptation, and it was not unusual for such girls to eventually marry and bear children.

With the male child the aim was quite different and the processing much more rigid. It was intended to be irreversible: but outright castration was seldom resorted to (only nineteen cases in the city in the year preceding Professor Stiel's report) and surgical removal of the ante-pituitary, though extremely effective, proved to be merely a passing vogue. Emotional conditioning, supplemented where necessary by drug treatment, was recognized as being so successful that all other methods were abandoned in its favor. So, having been dressed and addressed as a girl, encouraged to play with dolls as a preparation for impossible motherhood, taught only household tasks and otherwise feminized, the boygirl was married off at the age of about thirteen to a rich pederast. A dowry was paid to the parents and a strict contract drawn up ensuring the boygirl's financial security in the event of a divorce, which was in fact common. It is ironic that the very thoroughness of the boy-to-girl processing often foiled the mercenary motives behind it, for such was the resultant coquettishness and flightiness of many of the processees that they were unwilling to settle down with one man, or else it happened that their value on the marriage market was ruined by their reputations for promiscuity. In other cases feminization induced a narcissistic over-refinement and nourished a revulsion against the relatively coarse "opposite" sex for whom the boygirls were being prepared, which led them to prefer the company of their "own" sex and even to strike up pseudo-Lesbian relationships.

The above are extreme examples of course, and the term "doll people" refers not only to the completely reversed male and female but to the whole gamut of subtly merging heteroclites stretching between them.

TOOTS RACED up the stairs. One flight, two flights, three, four, five. Two flights to each storey. He clattered breathlessly upwards.

At each floor he glanced at the elevator indicator as he tore past, and he saw now that the light had slid up to four. They were close behind and gaining, but he had found his second wind. He rushed on. Now there was only one more flight to go. He took the steps three at a time.

Sixth floor. He halted beside the elevator doors and tried to get his breathing under control, and was standing there leaning against the wall in a not completely successful attempt at nonchalance when the doors slid apart and Malk, Sonny, Bobs and Ariston filed out. Toots grinned and held out his palm to Bobs.

—You lose again, mug. I told you I could beat you up.

—You look kind of beat-up yourself, Bobs grunted.

Toots snapped his fingers.

—C'mon. You owe.

Bobs grudgingly handed over some money and Toots shoved it into the back pocket of his jeans. Malk had been examining the various nameplates beside the doors. He turned to them.

—Looks like this is the one.

They clustered round him and read the nameplate. Dave Jacksall Enterprises Ltd.

—Press the buzzer, O leader, invited Sonny.

Malk did that little thing.

A rather synthetic-looking secretary opened to them. Malk nodded to her and they strolled in without a word and stood gazing about them.

The place was more like a luxury apartment than a suite of offices. From the deeply carpeted hallway ran a long corridor with four or five rooms opening on to it. The air was scented, and there was the soft pervasive sound of electronic music that was like a chromium-plated spiderweb made aural. The furniture, except for the business-like desk and steel filing cabinet (disapproving and keeping itself to itself), was expensively casual. As the group stood there a tousled young man, dressed in pajamas and carrying a towel, wandered sleepily out of one room and disappeared into another.

The secretary sat down behind the desk and raised her eyebrows inquiringly.

—We're expected, Malk muttered casually and glanced away from her.

She flicked a switch on the intercom.

—Your four o'clock appointment, Mr. Jacksall.

A ghost of a reply. She looked up with a sterile smile.

—The door right at the end of the corridor.

Malk nodded patronizingly, as though confirming she had got that right, drifted away, followed by the others.

The room at the end of the corridor was empty. Malk motioned the others to sit down and they slumped onto the divan and armchairs, all except Sonny, who toured about from wall to wall scrutinizing the abstract paintings and small sculptures. Malk helped himself to a cigarette from the box on the table in front of him and lit up. Bobs picked up a magazine and began to flick through it.

A tiny, almost dwarfish man had crept unnoticed into the room. He sat down on the divan beside Malk.

—Yes? he murmured ever so quietly.

Malk blinked at him.

—You Jacksall?

—Yes.

—Satiety Incorporated, Malk announced. —You asked us to come.

—Ah, yes.

Jacksall leaned back against the divan and glanced from one to the other. Sonny turned round from his examination of one of the canvasses.

—Nice daubings, he commented.

Jacksall gave a weak smile.

—I'm glad you approve.

—Do them yerself, did you? Toots inquired innocently.

Jacksall kept the smile on his face. He picked up the cigarette-box and waved it slowly about in a vague gesture of hospitality.

—Got one, thanks, said Malk, raising his hand to prove the obvious. —Let's get down to business, shall we?

Jacksall removed a cigarette and lit is as carefully as though it was his first ever.

—I've seen you boys a couple of times, he said, breathing out smoke. —I like your style.

—Our style? echoed Bobs.

Jacksall nodded.

—He likes our style, said Toots. —Yippee for us.

—Ignore them, said Malk.

—Yeah, ignore us, go on, said Toots.

Jacksall coughed delicately into his fist.

—You've worked on your own so far, haven't you? No manager?

Malk nodded. Jacksall tilted towards him as though fearing his light words might float away ceilingward before communicating his meaning.

—I'd like to manage you, he confided. —I can fix you with plenty of good bookings.

—We're doing all right without a manager, said Bobs.

Malk gave him a glance that told him to shut up.

—You'd do even better with one, Jacksall assured them. —How much do you get a night?

Malk didn't exaggerate, thinking that Jacksall had probably checked up and knew already.

—I can do better than that for you, sighed Jacksall. —Much better. I can get you on at bigger venues. Straight away, that is. Later, the biggest. Right away you'd be making at least five times what you're getting just now at these small clubs.

—Minus what? asked Malk.

—My share is fifty per cent.

—And a pint of blood a day? added Sonny.

—Yeah, you can forget it, said Malk. —That's way too much.

Toots slapped himself on the forehead.

—How can anyone say "My share is fifty per cent" and not blush?

Jacksall smiled, undisturbed.

—Even with my commission deducted you'd still be making more than double what you are now. And that's only a start. Of course I pay for new gear, your transport, all expenses.

All expenses. Malk liked the sound of that but pulled down the corners of his mouth sourly to hide his interest.

—It's still too much.

—Then there's publicity, Jacksall went on. —I intend to build you up. With the right exposure I could take you to the top. But that costs, and I pay for it all. So you see, I'm not being unreasonable.

—Oh, no, said Toots. —In fact we'd be ashamed to let you do it for so little, wouldn't we, Malk? How about offering him more – like a hundred per cent, maybe?

—Shut up, said Malk.

While Toots had been talking Jacksall had pressed a button on the table. The secretary came in and handed him a sheaf of papers. He passed them to Malk.

—I'm not asking for a decision now. Read these and let me know what you think.

Malk stuffed the contract into his pocket and they all stood up.

—See you, breathed Jacksall as the secretary showed them out.

—Not if we see you first, said Toots.

They left, sank down in the elevator, drifted out into the street and along to a bar.

—Maybe we should go further away before we talk about anything, Sonny suggested as they were about to go in. —This place is too near that creep's pad – he's probably got it bugged.

—Don't get all paranoid, soothed Toots. —It'll do.

They went in, settled around a corner table. A waiter took their order and brought the drinks.

—Well, what d'you think, Malk? Toots asked.

—Just what I said. His percentage is too high.

—D'you think he'll bring it down?

—He'd better. Down to twenty-five. Then we'll sign.

—I still don't see why we need a manager, said Bobs. —Why bother with this bloodsucker?

—Because he knows the business backwards, Malk answered. —Been in it years. I've checked him out. He's got the experience, he's got the money to back us, he's got the right connections.

He pulled out the contract and began to read it.

Sonny, Toots and Bobs gabbled on. Ariston wasn't listening to what they were saying. He didn't try to follow the conversation, just watched their faces, watched the skin around the mouth and eyes tighten, crinkle, pucker, as they talked and laughed. For him the afternoon had floated past, everything happening as though at a speed slightly less than normal, and now things were slowing down more and more. He watched Sonny lift his glass to drink. He saw the hand clutching it (fingers and tendons drawn by some superb artist) rise gradually to the readying mouth. Nearer, nearer. Then the red nether lip kissed the pale edge of the tilting glass, fastening on to it with sucker-like tenacity. The Adam's apple floated up and down under the smooth skin of the throat.

Suddenly Ariston rose and, without a word or look at them, left.

—Hey, where does creepo think he's off to? Bobs asked, not expecting an answer.

Malk raised his eyes from the contract and they all watched as Ariston walked away.

—Doesn't matter, Malk said, returning his attention to the contract. —As long as he turns up on time tonight.

Bobs, still staring after Ariston, shook his head.

—That one's a real case, he said. —But what I don't understand is the way the birds fancy him.

—One supposes, supposed Sonny sweetly, that the reason is that he's a good shaft. Better'n you.

—How would you know? Bobs mocked, and took a drink. He turned to Malk. —I mean, that night you brought him along, he really *stank* – the smell of him almost knocked you over! How could any bird fancy having it off with a stinking creep like that?

—How little you understand the opposite sex, sighed Toots.

—Nothing to understand, said Bobs. —It's a mistake to think there is. Birds are mindless – just cunt on legs.

Toots nodded.

—True. But that doesn't change the fact that they fancy him. Fancied him right from the word go, didn't they?

Bobs drank and said nothing.

—Don't suppose he's a shade jealous, do you? Sonny asked, leaning forward a little to speak past Bobs to Toots.

—What're you talking about? said Bobs. —There's always plenty of pussy. More than we need. I get my share and some of yours too.

—You're welcome, Sonny murmured.

—No, it's not that Bobsie boy here is jealous or anything like that, said Toots. —It's just that he's green with envy.

—Choked, agreed Sonny. —That's what he is. Choked.

—Why don't you go and cut yourself with a rusty razor? Bobs suggested. —He gives me the creeps, that's all.

—Tone it down, you lot, Malk complained. —I'm trying to make some sense out of this legal gibberish.

They ignored him.

—There was Bobs, you see, Toots went on, doing the singing bit, the plucking of the guitar bit, the swiveling hips bit – the swinging raver bit an' all that, in fact – and there were the birdies crowding round an' doing their tiny nuts an' yelling an' screaming an' then along comes smelly Ariston, phallic and aphrodisiacal – dig that crazy phrase! – an' makes them wet their panties with the thrill of it all an' steals them all away from Bobsie-wobsie. Aw, ain't it sad?

—Up yours, said Bobs.

Sonny winked at Toots.

—Remember that party last week? Sixteen birds he had in his room all night and every one of them with a satisfied look on her face in the morning.

Malk folded up the contract, put it away.

—We've been on the up and up since he joined us, he said, and it looks as though he's here to stay. So you'd better get along with him.

Bobs shrugged.

—I'm not denying what he's done for the band. It's just that he's too weird for words. Look at the way he slips away all the time. I mean, one minute you're talking to him, then you turn around an' there he is – gone!

—So what? said Sonny. —Maybe he thinks you stink too, in a different way.

—Listen, man, I could tell you something about him that would make you sick. It made *me* sick when I found out – I mean *literally* sick.

—Go on, then, urged Toots. —We're listening. Give us the dirt.

—You wouldn't believe it if I told you.

—We'll decide whether to believe it or not, said Malk. —Just tell us what it is.

—All right, all right. But you won't believe it, Bobs repeated.

He took a drink from his glass before beginning.

—Note the artful psychological touch, observed Sonny. —The pause by which the story-teller builds up the right atmosphere in his audience.

Bobs put down his glass and began.

—Well, as I said, I always thought there was something weird about him and I was curious to find out where he kept disappearing to. So one afternoon last week I followed him. He took a taxi across town. I came a bit behind in the van, parked when the taxi stopped, then followed him from there on foot.

Toots noisily sucked air in through his teeth.

—Man, this is surely exciting. Hey, know what, Bobs? You could've been a detective!

—Shut it, Malk told him mechanically.

—Where'd he go? Sonny asked.

—The rubbish dump.

—*Where?*

—You're having us on!

—Rubbish dump, Bobs repeated. —Went wandering away among the heaps of garbage. With me keeping well behind. Maybe too much behind. I lost him. So I climbed to the top of this great pile of junk, looked around. Saw him right away. Not far. He had stopped an' was standing still, crouched over, his back to me. Then he hunkered down, seemed to be looking at something. I started down towards him, not exactly noiselessly, but he didn't notice me, even as I came near. But then he must have heard me. Suddenly he whirled round, looked straight at me. I just stared. Didn't understand what I was seeing. It was his mouth – it was smeared with stuff … gunge – I dunno, some kind of filthy muck. Some on his hands as well. I just couldn't believe he'd actually been eating it, whatever it was, but he must've been. It took a couple of seconds for the fact to sink in, then I was sick on the spot, just bent over and retched till my stomach was empty. And when I straightened up he was gone.

Bobs picked up his drink and finished it off in one, as though to cleanse his throat of the memory.

—And now tell me you believe me.

THE ATMOSPHERE in the crematorium chapel of the Last Exit funeral parlor was hushed and solemn, as befitted the occasion. The mortal remains of Pete, which for some weeks had lain unidentified in a deep-freeze slot in the morgue, were about to be subjected to the opposite extreme of temperature. Pete's dad and weepy mum had already taken a long last look at the face of their beloved son (rouged, powdered, beautiful in death) and the coffin lid was being screwed down by the chapel attendants.

Dad leaned confidentially towards the mortician.

−I think you did a fine job on him, he mumbled, with a nod towards the coffin. −Real wonderful, I calls it. Made him look quite human, you did.

The mortician acknowledged the compliment with a dignified nod. He himself was a zombie-like creature and might have been taken as a walking paradigm of his own art.

−Thank you, he murmured. −Every corpse has *something*, you know, *some* special quality or other; we try to bring that out.

−Yes, sniffed mum, it was a nice touch, having him holding a guitar like that – even though he was actually a drummer.

The mortician's already stiff manner stiffened even more, as if his perception that mum's innocent compliment contained a hint of criticism had brought on a further degree of rigor mortis.

−We were of course fully aware of that, he enounced carefully. −But we thought a drum kit would be rather cumbrous in a coffin. Drumsticks just by themselves, though representative, would have been too *slight* – besides which, they looked just a bit like chopsticks when I tried that idea out.

–I can see you went to a lot of trouble, said mum, trying to make amends.

The mortician paid no attention.

–The musical motif, he went on, that's what was important. The particular instrument used was of no great significance, I think you'll agree.

–Oh, I do, I do, mum agreed eagerly.

–Our policy, said the mortician, somewhat soothed, is to aim at an aesthetic balance between unimaginative truth and frivolous embellishment.

–A lovely job, said dad. –You made a lovely job of him.

Now, as Ariston sat at the drums and gently tapped out a somber rhythm, the coffin was lifted by Malk, Bobs, Sonny and Toots, carried forward (rather at a tilt due to the considerable differences in their heights) and reverently placed on the conveyor that in a minute or so would trundle it into the furnace. It was to be a quiet ceremony – hardly a ceremony at all really, just a few words read out by the mortician from an anthology of orations while Satiety Incorporated provided a touching musical background in the form of a slow blues number.

The mortician opened his anthology. That was the signal. A switch was depressed and the conveyor started. The group played, humming spiritually, and the mortician began to recite the archaic and solemn but not particularly intelligible passage he had chosen. The furnace doors gaped wide as the coffin neared them. Mum wept, sniffing noisily, and dad put his arm round her shoulders.

Just then there was a mild commotion at the back of the chapel. Seven or eight girls pattered in. They stood bunched nervously together, whispering, glancing at the band and the coffin and then looking away and tittering.

Malk gave Bobs a dirty look, growled out of the corner of his mouth at him.

–Didn't I tell you to park the van well away from here? Bloody hopeless, you are.

Bobs shrugged.

One of the attendants went up to the girls and motioned them to sit down. Obediently, though still whispering, they settled in a pew. After putting a finger to his pursed lips to emphasize the desirability for silence, the attendant tiptoed back to his post. The service continued undisturbed. Then the coffin passed into the inferno and the furnace doors closed behind it. At the same time the mortician drew his recitation to a close.

Meanwhile more girls had been sneaking in. There were about thirty now. All at once a bunch of twenty or so arrived, pushing its way noisily through the swing doors. They were wilder than the earlier gatecrashers, more excited, and their excitement immediately infected the others. Those who had been sitting down stood up. They all started to whisper and giggle. There were a few tentative screams, a few oohs and aahs, and with a sinister slowness the girls began to filter down the aisle between the pews towards the group.

The mortician and his two minions hurriedly blocked their path.

−Please, the mortician pleaded, his arms outspread. −Some respect, please. I must ask you to remember where you are.

Only one or two of the girls bothered trying to push past them. The rest simply clambered over the pews.

−Ariston! some called, their round, mesmerized eyes focused on the object of their devotion. −Oh, Ariston!

−Sonny! others shouted. −Sonnee!

−Bobs!

−Toots!

−Malk! Malk!

The boys had stopped playing. They stood motionless and watching the approaching fans.

−For some reason I feel just a shade nervous, said Sonny, swallowing.

−Don't lose your cool, said Bobs. −It's all ri−

He jumped as a girl he hadn't noticed come up on his right suddenly clutched hold of his sleeve. He jerked his arm free and gave her a strained smile.

−Coming to see us tonight, then, love?

She nodded vigorously.

−Ooh, yeah, Bobs. Wouldn't miss ya.

Another girl thrust an autograph book at him. He scribbled his name in it and handed it back.

−Can I have yer tie as well? asked the autograph-hunter. −Yeah? Can I?

Her fingers were already gripping the tie. A girl beside her snatched at it, the two of them began to squabble.

−Let me have it – you got his autograph!

−Get yer hands off. Go on, beat it!

Each held on to the tie with one hand and pushed and clawed at her rival with the other, tugging Bobs to and fro in the process. His face was turning crimson.

−HEY! he shouted, jerking the tie away from them. −You trying to throttle me?

He stepped back, loosening the tie and flung it to them. There was a general scramble.

−C'mon, said Sonny. −Let's get out of here – like *now*!

A fan had settled herself on Ariston's knee. She had slipped her hand under his shirt and was kissing his face and neck. Two others rushed up and hauled her off, and immediately began to fight over who was to take her place. The last semblance of order had gone but Ariston just sat there as though this had nothing much to do with him.

−Please, the mortician could still be heard wailing. −Some RESPECT!

Malk swiftly slipped his guitar off, rammed it into a fan's face, grabbed hold of Ariston and yanked him to his feet.

−Everyone out! he shouted, fighting off fans. −The side door!

−What about the gear? Toots yelled.

−Leave it!

−Excuse us, said Toots, pushing away a couple of screaming, clinging admirers. −Back in five minutes, girls.

Malk made them keep close together and with the help of the attendants they managed to force their way to the side exit.

—Sorry about all this, Bobs called to mum and dad on his way out.

Dad waved the apology aside.

—We understand, he called back. —That's showbiz.

—Yeah, you're right there.

At last they were outside the funeral parlor and inside the van. Malk sounded the horn and revved the engine furiously to warn off the girls who were hanging on the doors and trying to climb onto the roof and bonnet. Then they were away, racing down the street.

—I think there must've been one lying under the wheels, commented Toots, gazing out of the rear windows. —There's a nasty red blotch back there on the road.

—Never mind them, said Malk. —Are you lot all in one piece?

There was a chorus of grunts and yeahs.

—Hey, you've lost some of yer hair, Ariston, my boy, said Bobs.

Ariston put up his hand and felt where a fan had torn a hank of his long mane from above the left temple.

—Worry not, advised Toots. —You can comb your hair so your bald patch won't show.

—We were lucky to get off so lightly, mumbled Sonny. —They were after our blood. I knew it. Knew it. Soon as I saw them I just knew it.

—Yeah, we're getting really popular, Toots chortled. —Where's the record now, anyway? Last I heard, it was at twenty-two.

—In the top twenty now, Bobs told him. —Early this afternoon it was at eighteen.

Toots rubbed his hands.

—That's what I like to hear, man. All that lovely money – it makes me feel warm and cosy just to think about it.

—Hey, Malk.

—What?

—When're we going to go back for the gear?

Malk chuckled.

—Gear? What gear? Those fans'll've shredded it for souvenirs. Naw, we'll just charge the cost of new gear to Jacksall. It'll set him back a packet, all right, but he should worry, considering the kind of money we're bringing him in now.

—Yeah, Sonny agreed. —And then, he'll squeeze a lot of free publicity out of this. In fact, it wouldn't surprise me if he arranged the whole thing. Just the kind of stunt his twisted mind would conjure up.

THE VIOLENT incident at the crematorium had not in fact been engineered by the manager-agent of Satiety Incorporated. It was an entirely spontaneous outbreak of adulation, the first of a series of emotional happenings of geometrically increasing virulence and intensity which were to build up to a peak of fetid hysteria such as had never before been encountered even in that black-magic city. However, though he hadn't staged the initial mobbing, Jacksall (as Sonny had anticipated) saw to it that the most effective possible use was made of the event publicity-wise. He knew his job, and had good reason to be pleased with the media coverage given his boys on that occasion – and he made sure there were others, arranging for the band to be swamped and manhandled by raving fans on its next half-dozen appearances. After that there was no need for fakery. The mania began to feed on itself and whenever yet another incident involving Satiety Incorporated hit the media – which happened more and more frequently – it was due to the entirely genuine frenzy of an unpaid mob. The phenomenal surge of feverish popularity delighted Jacksall, but he believed it to be only a hint of things to come.

—You're going to be the greatest ever, he prophesied in his loudest whisper. —You're going to be big, *big*, BIG!

—But are we going to be alive, *alive*, ALIVE!? queried Sonny, who had fared particularly badly in the fans' last show of enthusiasm. —Man, those people out there are real vicious!

—Yella belly, Bobs sneered. —Little baby'll be having nightmares next.

—I'm having nightmares already, Sonny confessed unashamedly. —You would too, if you weren't so thick.

The two began to throw a few well-chosen insults at each other. They and the others had been summoned to Jacksall's office suite for a pep talk. With the exception of the nervously hunched-forward Sonny, the boys sat sprawled about in the chairs much as they had done on their first visit there, with the same ease and self-assurance but with more of it.

Malk turned to Jacksall.

—Sonny's imagination is in overdrive but there's something in what he says. Things are becoming just a tad too savage for my liking.

Jacksall held up his hands, palms out.

—There's not a thing to worry about, he said soothingly. —Don't I always look after you? Now just hold on a minute. I've got a little present for you.

Leaning forward, he murmured into the intercom.

—Woolgar, would you send them in?

A few seconds later the secretary opened the door and, an apprehensive expression on her face, stood holding it wide open while into the room lumbered five humanoid behemoths. All were over six feet nine and proportionately broad and gave the impression they might weigh half a ton each.

The band gaped.

—Bodyguards, Jacksall announced with a touch of pride, as though they were bespoke creations. —One each.

—I'm speechless with gratitude, said Toots. —I am really, but just think of the grocery bills! Anyway, the ceilings in my pad are just a shade on the low side.

Jacksall coughed lightly into his fist.

—They're professional wrestlers, he said. —Toughest in the business. You're going to be in one another's company a lot from now on, so I hope you'll all be friends.

—I wouldn't dream of being enemies, said Bobs.

Jacksall nodded.

—Good, good, said Jacksall, nodding and rubbing his hands. —Well, boys, there are some papers to be signed. After that, you'd better get straight along to the recording studio.

When the signing was over the band, accompanied by its bodyguard, trooped down to the parking lot, climbed into the new minibus (replacing the one fans had destroyed two days ago) and were driven to the studio by Al, the road manager (who, being elsewhere at the time of the death of the previous minibus, had been lucky not to share its fate). He had already delivered the boys' gear and together with the producer had set up the equipment; everything was ready and waiting and on arrival the group set straight to work.

Two hours later four numbers had been recorded. The producer told them to take a break but to be back in a half-hour to do two more. After that they would be finished for the day.

—Use the company restaurant, he told them from his booth, his voice reaching them through their headphones. —On the top floor. And remember, don't go outside. I don't want a load of little scrubbers following you back.

—Yessir, said Bobs. —Anything you say.

—*Twit*, he added under his breath.

They quit the studio and walked along to the elevator. The towering wrestlers followed close behind. The elevator doors opened and the boys got in.

—I think you darlings better not crowd us, Toots said to the bodyguards and pointed to the maximum-weight notice. —We'll see you up there. Cheerio.

The giants accepted this with no reaction, stood passively as the elevator doors closed on them, stood waiting.

But the elevator went down, not up, down to the ground floor. The group emerged, crossed the foyer and went out of the building.

—Freedom! said Bobs.

—Ah, outside air! exulted Toots, breathing deep the odors of the street. —It's not natural, that drycleaned stuff they use in there.

They walked on, exchanging grumbles, letting off steam.

—That producer gent is a pain in the brain, Malk commented.

—Yeah, agreed Sonny. —And the same goes for our mighty mammoths. I feel as though I'm being shadowed by a range of mountains.

They had come to the end of the block.

—We're too obvious together, said Malk. —Better split before we're recognized.

—Okay, said Toots. —See you back at the studio. C'mon, Bobs.

They went off together to the right. Malk and Sonny walked straight on. Ariston, left by himself, cut down the street to his left.

Malk glanced back over his shoulder at him.

—Hardly a fucking word out of him since he joined the group, he muttered. —Bobs is right – he's a nutter.

—Aren't we all? Sonny asked. —The question is, what kind of nutter is he?

Malk shrugged.

—A nutter who can play the drums, he answered. —So who cares, anyway? C'mon, let's get a bite to eat.

It was almost an hour later before they were all back at the recording studio. There had been no trouble with fans. None of them had even been recognized, except Ariston, who'd been trailed to the glass doors of the building by a posse of girls from offices and shops or who had just been passing by on the street and had stopped passing by. After he'd disappeared inside, they loitered about on the sidewalk, their numbers growing as the news of the band's whereabouts spread. Up on the eighth floor the session continued. The fifth and sixth songs were recorded, then when they thought they could go, the producer held them back.

—That fourth one you did earlier, he told them. —It's all right as it is, but I've been thinking about it and know how we could do it just that little bit better.

—*We*? queried Toots. —Since when did you join this merry band of strollers?

—If it wasn't for me you'd sound like a bunch of castrated alley cats, came the bored voice from the booth.

—Go and re-mix yourself, suggested Bobs.

—Just shut up, said Malk, and let's get on with it.

They listened while the producer told them how he wanted the song done this time. With only minor changes, it didn't take long to get it as he thought it should be.

—Okay, that'll do, he said when he was satisfied. —You were a shade weak on the ending, but I got a good take of that earlier so I'll just do a little transplant and everything'll be fine. You may go now.

—Oh, *may* we *really*, your baldness? mocked Bobs and was about to add to that when, with a splitting noise the big double studio doors burst open, banged against the walls, and a spate of girls, an endless flooding, screaming stream of them that swept the giant bodyguards in front of it like uprooted trees, flooded in and rushed straight for the band.

—Where've they come from? screamed the voice from the sound booth. —Get them out of my studio, get them OUT!

The lads were already running for the exit at the other side of the studio. They would have been well away if Sonny, made clumsy by panic, hadn't tangled himself in the lead from his guitar. In a flash the shrieking girls had piled onto him. With a piteous yelp he sank under them. Malk and Bobs, kicking and punching, dived into the heap of writhing bodies and heaved him bodily out. There was a long ripping noise as his shirt was torn from his back. His stack-heeled boots, one sock and his jeans were lost in the brief but ferocious tug-of-war. But he was free. Half-naked, he raced out of the studio. Still punching and kicking mercilessly in a rearguard action, Malk and Bobs kept the fans at bay as they backed slowly to the door. Once in the corridor outside, they turned and belted down to where the others were waiting in the elevator, holding the doors open for them. They stumbled in. The lift doors began to shut, managed it only just before the mob reached them. The boys took the elevator down to the basement and escaped by the back of the building.

That evening they watched footage showing how the frustrated worshippers had rampaged through the recording studio to leave it looking like a twice-used battlefield. From souvenir-hunting fans they had transmogrified into a gang of wreckers – it seemed there had been something almost systematic the way they had left nothing destructible intact. The sound booth had been tough enough to withstand the repeated assaults on it, but the producer, barricaded inside, had gone through a nightmarish half-hour before the horde had withdrawn. His nerves had been so badly affected that he had been carted off to a clinic for sedation and a long rest. The recordings, Jacksall phoned to tell them, had been saved.

—They'll get us one day, Sonny muttered, staring at a screen showing the ruined studio. —It's fate. They'll get us one day.

CONSIDER CHEESE. That's simple enough, now, isn't it? It's a straightforward food and a healthy food. You get a fair deal with cheese. You can't go wrong with it. Now, it's interesting how they make cheese, sir. I mean, for example, did you know the rennin used for coagulating the milk is obtained from the fourth stomach of unweaned calves? Of course, it's made all over the world and comes in all shapes and sizes, as you no doubt realize. A famous philosopher once said: "If it wasn't for cheese, life would be very different." No-one could refute him on that point. They were silent and thought about it for a while, then they agreed. No, it doesn't do to underestimate cheese. It's full of protein. That means goodness. The moon, you know, was once reputed to be made out of cheese. Of course those were the days of superstition and ignorance and the composition of that satellite is now known to be of a less nutritious order. Cheese, I may say, is the last of the unadulterated foodstuffs. The experts haven't yet found a way to make it more marketable, so it remains edible. ...

Ariston nodded. Rats and mice aren't so stupid. That's why they take a bit of cheese when they can get it. They know what's good for them. He knew the rats knew what was good for them; after all, he'd lived with them. They were his friends. That's why he was buying the stuff for them. He paid cash and had the cheeses loaded into the grocer's van and taken to the rubbish dump. A farewell gift. For old times' sake.

He hadn't bought the fancy kinds. None of your yak-milk cheese, no water buffalo or llama cheeses here, thank you very much. Rats had unsophisticated tastes, so good, homely cheeses were the order of the day. But plenty of them. Ariston told the two shop assistants who'd brought the cheeses to distribute them appetizingly around the dump.

When that had been done he sent the men away in the van. As he had tipped them generously they were careful not to laugh at him to his face. They made signs behind his back and smothered their sniggers like kids in class, but once inside the van they let themselves go. They drove off shouting comments and guffawing. They laughed so much on their way back into town that the driver lost control; the van crashed and they were both killed. The accident was too insignificant to earn a mention in the next day's media.

Chewing some cheese (to show it wasn't poisoned), Ariston waited for the rats to make an appearance. But none came. He waited, waited, waited. He couldn't understand it. They were his friends. He was their friend. He stayed as long as he could but there was a practice and he couldn't miss it. Walking sadly away, he hoped the cheeses wouldn't go to waste.

At the first phone booth he came to he called for a taxi. He felt very lonely. From the back of the taxi he stared out unseeingly and passed the burnt-out van and attendant ambulance and police car without noticing them.

—Where the hell have you been? Malk shouted when he arrived. —You're pissing late!

Without a word Ariston took up his drumsticks and began to play.

THE SEATING capacity of the city sports stadium was two hundred thousand, but on the evening Satiety Incorporated had been booked to play there, at a fee of half a million dollars for a one-hour performance, at least twenty thousand additional fans had illegally gained admittance. Tickets had been forged, tunnels had been dug under the perimeter wall (one tunnel collapsing and burying several fans alive). Every imaginable type of ruse had been resorted to at the entrance gates, sometimes with success, sometimes not.

The warm-up act was on stage. A mile away, in the hotel suite the band was using as headquarters and hideaway for that evening, the noise of the crowd could be heard clearly.

—They sound really hungry tonight, commented Toots as he stood by the window gazing out at the glittering panorama of city lights.

Jacksall scowled at him, then threw a worried glance at Sonny, who was pacing up and down the lounge carpet. But it didn't look as though he had heard.

Sonny hadn't. He was too preoccupied with the whisperings of his own fear, which was capable of much more grisly and vivid insinuations than Toots was.

—It's tonight. Tonight they're going to get us, Sonny mumbled to himself as he prowled backwards and forwards. —I can feel it. I know it, I just know it. ...

Jacksall flipped his wrist and read the time. Forty-three minutes till blast-off, he thought, and this inbred bastard has to start breaking up.

—Can't you stop that walking up and down all the time? said Malk. —What's got into you, anyway?

—Shut up! Sonny snapped. —Just leave me alone – and that goes for all of you!

Jacksall came forward, reached up to put a hand on Sonny's shoulder.

—Why don't you lie down for a bit? he suggested, steering him towards the open door of a bedroom. Sonny didn't resist.

In the bedroom, as Jacksall was closing the door, he flopped onto the bed and curled up into the fetal position.

—Help me, he whimpered to no-one in particular. —Help me.

His manager sat down on the edge of the bed.

—You're getting yourself all worked up over nothing, kid, soothed Jacksall, his smile as smooth and viscous as syrup. —Everything'll be okay, I tell you – and your bodyguard'll be standing by, just in case.

Instantly, as though Jacksall's words had been some kind of a Pavlovian signal, Sonny went into convulsions. His body rocked tightly from side to side and his legs, jerking out straight in a vigorous spasm, swept his manager off the bed and onto the floor, while shrieks of mirthless laughter issued from his mouth.

—Five, he wheezed and gasped, his eyes glittering with feverish sarcasm. —Five against a couple of hundred thousand! That's very reassuring! Oh, that makes everything just fine!

He was overcome with a second attack of twitches and jolts.

—No, no. You don't understand, said Jacksall patiently as he picked himself up and dusted off his sharkskin suit. —I've hired dozens more especially for tonight's performance. And half the police force will be there.

—The cops! shrieked Sonny. —They hate us! They hate us for shafting their daughters. I know them – they'll deliberately let the fans get at us. ...

He ranted on and on until his fingers, which had been plucking fitfully at the green bedcover, began stuffing it into his mouth, choking down the vomit of words. Jacksall, gazing down at the shuddering figure on the bed, was forced to admit to himself that outside assistance was required. He reached for the phone.

—Is there a doctor in the hotel? I need one up here right away.

The hotel had its own medical adviser: he and the hotel manager were at the door of the suite in two minutes. Jacksall took the doctor by the elbow and outlined the situation as he led him to the bedroom.

—Sounds as though he needs an alienist, said the doctor. —Not really my field.

—Just fix him up for tonight, Jacksall pleaded. —That's all I ask. Tomorrow I'll call in the best psychiatrist money can buy.

The doctor grunted.

—Well, let's have a look at this young man.

The hotel manager held the bedroom door open for him and they went in. Sonny lay curled up on the bed rambling quietly to himself.

—Sonny, Jacksall whispered. —Someone to see you. ...

—Go away, Sonny moaned, not bothering to open his eyes. —I'm not going on stage tonight and no-one can make me. Shan't. Won't.

—What seems to be the trouble? asked the doctor, taking the patient's wrist.

Sonny jerked his arm away.

—Don't touch me! he hissed.

He scuttled to the far end of the bed and began hoisting the bedclothes over his head.

—Get out – all of you get out! he shouted. —I won't go on, I won't, I won't. ...

His voice became muffled as he succeeded in raising a floppy sort of tent over himself. Bobs and Toots, standing in the doorway, were watching unsympathetically.

—Hey, Sonny, just cut it out! You trying to louse us all up?

—Yeah, this is our big night!

There was a suffocated but recognizably impolite response from under the clothes. Jacksall went over to Bobs and Toots and assured them that it would be all right, then shut the door on them. The doctor had broken a glass phial and was filling a hypodermic. While Jacksall and the hotel manager held Sonny down he rubbed a swab up and down on the skin of his inner forearm and slipped the needle expertly into a vein.

—Hold him just a few seconds more, he told them when he'd given the injection.

Sonny struggled for half a minute, then dropped back onto the bed as though sledgehammered.

—But look at him! exclaimed Jacksall, eyeing the unconscious guitarist. —He's out cold! You sure you haven't overdone it, doc?

The doctor snapped his black bag shut.

—The initial effect will wear off in fifteen or twenty minutes. After that he'll wake up refreshed and be quite calm.

Jacksall continued to fuss.

—He'll be able to play? You're sure?

Feeling it below his professional dignity to answer, the doctor dismissed the matter and Jacksall with a curt nod and left, followed by the hotel manager.

Almost twenty minutes later Sonny woke. He was, as the doctor had foretold, peaceful, though his manner was rather absent and Jacksall was still worried about whether he would be able to play or not.

As it turned out, it wouldn't have mattered if none of them had been able to play, for at the first moment of their appearance in the stadium the constant screaming of the fans swelled to a great bestial chaos of sound and at that mindbending, chord- and word-drowning level it remained unabated throughout the performance.

From the concrete exit of the underground changing-rooms the group walked quickly across the floodlit expanse of grass and skipped up the steps to the platform (which was surrounded by a palisade of Jacksall's specially selected stalwarts). Almost at once the boys were ready to play, and stood fidgeting as they waited for the noise to drop. The fans kept right on screaming. Malk held up his arms and appealed for quiet, shouting into his mike in a futile attempt to make himself heard. Then he gave a shrug and turned to the others.

—Okay, here we go. A-four, a-three, a-two, a-one!

They launched into the act. No-one heard them. Like figures in a silent movie they plucked their guitars, mouthed and gaped, stamped, shook, gesticulated. Girls and doll people collapsed in orgasmic ecstasies and were carried off on stretchers. Feverish and sweating, as though infected by the crowd, the boys were belting through the songs.

Wilder and wilder grew the pace and when Sonny, relapsing into hysteria in spite of the sedative, smashed his instrument to pieces and hurled away the bits, began to tear off his clothes and scratch his face, the fans took it all as part of the performance. They smelled blood, and howled for more.

Between the stage and the spectators were two hundred yards of grass, an area no fan had as yet attempted to cross without being captured by the police and led or lifted away. But now a whole section of the audience suddenly surged forward as one. The wire-mesh fence that separated the sports pitch from the seating area was flattened (at the cost of the lives of two girls and a doll, who were crushed into the mesh or against the steel posts) and the fans poured out through the breach. The police no longer bothered to try to effect captures but simply drew their clubs and lashed out left, right and centre. Fans with bloodied heads dropped stunned to the ground. Scores fell. But there were hundreds more streaming through the gap.

Inside Sonny something sagged in a complete abnegation. When a nightmare comes true there is no longer any point in struggling against it. Eyes glazed, he jumped from the stage, easily avoided the clumsy attempts of the surprised bodyguards to restrain him and rushed open-armed towards his bloodbeasts. He must have screamed as the first claws fastened on him, but his voice was lost among so many others. In a moment he had been engulfed.

Ariston still sat at his drums, the sticks held loosely in his hands. He didn't know what to do. Everything was happening too quickly. He was too confused to move. Shouting at him to follow, Malk, Bobs and Toots had run down from the platform and were already almost half-way to the exit tunnel. As he glanced after their retreating backs he saw them slow down, hesitate, then stop. A second section of the audience, the one flanking the exit, had downed the perimeter fence and broken through the police cordon. The three would-be escapees paled as a horde of screaming harpies flew towards them. The way out was sealed. There was nothing they could do but turn and race back for the stage.

They didn't make it. They had hesitated a little too long before heading back. Fans converged on them from all sides. Bobs slipped on the grass and went down, almost immediately disappearing under a pile of bodies. A few yards farther on Malk and Toots were dragged to a halt and met the same fate. At that moment there was a vivid blue flash, a sharp explosion. The stadium arc-lamps went out, and from that point the proceedings continued illuminated only by the baleful light of the moon.

It was Ariston's turn next. The bodyguard had remained faithfully in position and, backed up by a mustering of police, had succeeded in keeping the stage clear of fans; but now even this island fortress was about to fall to the teenage berserkers.

It was then, when death seemed inevitable, that Ariston felt gusts of wind. Looking up, he saw a helicopter hovering about seventy feet above him. Because its engine noise was absorbed by the screaming and howling of the crowd it appeared to be floating up there quite silently, and as it was only half visible in the moonlight the general effect was unreal. But the white rope-ladder that dropped from the aircraft's belly was real enough, its end hanging about ten feet above Ariston's head. Skillfully the helicopter was lowered so that the ladder dangled right beside him. Ariston grabbed hold of a rung with first one hand, then both, then hugged the swaying ladder to him. Immediately the helicopter rose.

The last line of defense had broken. Fans rushed for Ariston, their rapacious little paws reaching for him. Just too late, failing, only just failing, to seize their sacrificial idol. Ariston soared up and away, well beyond their uplifted arms, and from their contorted red mouths below came a great half-sob, half-shriek of disappointment and despair.

AT FIRST Ariston dared not, could not, move a muscle. His hands gripped the rope-ladder with a fierce rigidity, one thought only in his mind – he must not try to climb up, must not move at all, or he would slip and fall. So, hugging the ladder tightly against his chest, not daring to look down, he drifted on above the rooftops. The moon watched with mild interest.

Onward he sailed. Gradually, as being hauled across the sky began to lose some of its novelty, he began to lose some of his fear. Courage, my friend, whispered the moon. Or was it the cold night air that whistled about his ears? Certainly the more he felt the air's chilling effects, the more he considered the idea of getting up to the inside of the helicopter. Cautiously he started lifting a foot up to the next rung. But he stopped, let his foot sink back onto the rung it had so foolishly ventured from, waited, drawing in and holding deep calming breaths. Easy does it, my friend, easy. In slow motion he tried again, felt the rung under his foot, shifted his weight onto it, began raising himself. Not so difficult. Another pause, then, still in slow motion, he stretched a hand up to grip the rung above the one it had been clenching. Pause. He brought his lower foot up to join the other, paused, brought up the other hand. Pause, up to the next rung. Up, rung by cautious rung, he went. His intense concentration left little space for feeling fear. His flight through the air was so smooth that climbing the flexible ladder, he found, was only slightly more awkward than if he had been on an ordinary ladder on solid ground. Making sure before each step upward that he had a firm grip with both hands, he crawled upwards.

As Ariston hauled himself into the cabin the pilot twisted round in his seat and grinned cheerfully.

—About time, mate, he called over his shoulder. —Pull the ladder up after you, there's a good fellow. And shut the hatch – it just slides forwards. Wouldn't do for you to drop out after all that trouble getting in, eh? Then come and squeeze in here, he added, nodding at the seat beside him.

Ariston lay on the floor recovering, looking at the pilot's back.

—You saved my life, he said.

The pilot waved the remark away.

—Don't mention it. Just sorry I couldn't wind you up – damn winch bust the other day and hasn't been fixed yet.

After a few minutes rest, Ariston pulled up the ladder, slid the hatch shut, then crawled towards the pilot on all fours and maneuvered himself into the seat beside him.

—What happened to your mates? the pilot asked.

—They've had it, I guess.

—Really? That's tough.

Ariston gazed out into the night.

—Nice view you get up here, he commented.

—Panoramic, that's the word, enthused the pilot. —The city lights, the sea – yeah, never get tired of it myself. I prefer flying at night, you know. Too much glare during the day.

—Well, I'm glad you happened to be out tonight, said Ariston.

The pilot chuckled.

—Yes, not a second too early, was I? But I didn't just *happen* to be there tonight at the crucial moment. Old Thingamy sent me to collect you.

—Thingamy?

—You *know*, said the pilot, screwing up his face in the effort to remember. —Old whatsisname – *Mackleford*, that's it! He got news what was happening at the stadium and sent me out for you. Pal of yours, is he?

—Never heard of him.

Ariston said nothing more for a minute, then asked:

—Where're we going now?

—His place, of course. Thingamy's.

The helicopter had crossed the city and reached the sea. For about ten minutes it followed the moonlit coastline, then began to lose height.

—Almost there, the pilot said. —See those lights? That's the house.

They approached the place from the landward side. The pilot had switched on a powerful floodlight that illuminated the area immediately beneath them and, looking down, Ariston saw that they were hovering over a spacious lawn. They began to descend.

—What am I supposed to do here? Ariston asked.

—Couldn't say, mate, answered the pilot. —I was hired to bring you. That's all I know.

A few minutes later Ariston was standing on the lawn watching the helicopter rise up and shrink away into the night. As the noise of its rotors faded he turned to the house.

Although lights were burning brightly on both floors there was no sign of life. The house was very still. The sound of waves came gently but clearly from the beach. Ariston listened a while and breathed in the sweet odors of the garden, until the hypnotic rhythm of the sea lured him from the lawn to a path that led along by the side of the house and down to the sand. The tide was flowing in. Waves spilled over the shore, grabbing, sucking, disintegrating in lathers of foam, while farther out fresh lines of assault hunched their backs and sallied in.

Along the beach, glistening in the moonlight like silver dolphins, two figures sported in the small surf. First Ariston heard their laughter; he turned his head in the direction it came from and then spotted them as they frisked through the breaking wash. A man and a woman. They seemed to be naked. Suddenly the woman turned towards the shore, waded clear of the waves and ran lithely off. Shouting, the man chased after her and they fled laughing into the deeper darkness of the farther beach.

Ariston went back to the house. The front door was ajar. He pushed it so that it swung wide open, hesitated, took a couple of steps inside, then paused again.

To his left an open staircase curved up to the next floor. To his right was a wide living-area sunken below the level of the hallway and reached by three wall-to-wall wooden steps. Ariston's gaze circled round and came to rest on a table near him; on top of the table was a bronze gong. He realized that anyone in the house must have heard the noise of the helicopter but he felt the need to announce himself, to break the stillness. He lifted the felt-tipped hammer and hit the gong hard. The sound reverberated through the house and gradually smoothed out into silence.

Ariston stepped down into the living-area. He strolled around restlessly, touching the rich fabrics and expensive woods of the luxuriously furnished room and examining its various ornaments and curios. Finally he lit a cigarette and sat down. There was nothing to do but wait.

IT WAS the sound of rain that woke him: but, sitting up and glancing at the windows, he saw there was no rain. At the same time he realized that the sound came from upstairs. Someone was taking a shower. He stood up.

The shower was turned off. Ariston heard a woman's voice humming. Footsteps slapped wetly along a floor. One neat slim-ankled foot, cut off from its body by the line of the ceiling, appeared on the top step of the stairway. Then came the other foot, then softly tanned calves, the hem of a white bathrobe and a glimpse of smooth thigh. Ariston saw her face first in profile, a sharp, nervous profile. She was two-thirds down the stairs before she sensed his presence, stopped and turned towards him, and he was surprised by the full lips, the wide, high-boned cheeks, the heavy sensuousness. She looked down at him with no sign of surprise or of any other reaction, and when she spoke her voice was low and controlled.

—Who are you?

—Ariston.

Now, her arched eyebrows rising almost imperceptibly, she did show some slight surprise or puzzlement.

—Ariston? ... The drummer?

—Yeah.

For a few moments she considered this, then continued down the stairs, her blue eyes never leaving his face. As she reached the bottom of the stairs she paused again.

—And you're here ... why? she asked.

He shrugged.

—Mackleford, he muttered.

—Mac? What about him?

—He sent for me.

—Did he now? Well, well. I wonder why.

Ariston shrugged again.

—That's what I'd like to know.

She gave him a wry smile.

—He has some good reason, of that I'm sure. We'll just have to wait and see what it is. Meanwhile you may as well make yourself comfortable. Go on, sit down. I was just going to make coffee – care for some?

—Sure. Thanks.

Still standing at the foot of the stairs, she went on watching him with the same feline calmness but now with a hint of amusement added. He sat down on the couch again and she turned and walked down a short corridor to the kitchen.

—By the way, she called back, when did you get here? About an hour ago?

—An hour? Maybe. Don't know. I fell asleep.

—So the helicopter, that was you?

—Yeah. It collected me.

From the kitchen came the sound of a laugh.

—*Collected* you?

Then there was the sound of water filling a kettle and the chink of cups and saucers. A radio was switched on; some pop music was followed by an announcer's voice. Ariston couldn't make out what was being said. After a few minutes the voice was cut off and the woman came back carrying a tray.

—Where is everyone? Ariston asked.

—Out, she answered simply.

—And you? he asked.

—Oh, I was out too, just for a while.

—Maybe it was you I saw down along the beach when I arrived.

As she bent forwards to put the tray on the table in front of him the lapels of her bathrobe fell open.

—Maybe it was, she said, sitting down beside him on the couch and starting to pour the coffee. She reached for a small metal jug. —Milk?

He shook his head. Passing him his coffee, she indicated a plate of sandwiches.

—Help yourself, she invited.

He took one, bit into it.

She watched him munch hungrily at it.

—I heard on the radio just now that your friends are all dead, she said, holding her cup in both hands. —In fact, they think you're dead too. Apparently there are all sorts of different reports going around. No-one seems to really know what happened.

—Well, they're wrong about me, anyway, he commented, chewing.

She sipped her coffee.

—Don't you care – about the others?

Ariston helped himself to another sandwich.

—Does anybody care about anybody?

She smiled.

—My, how cynical we are!

—Just glad I got out, that's all.

—Weren't you buddies and all that?

—They were buddies. I was on the outside looking in.

She tut-tutted.

—How too alienating for you.

He swallowed a mouthful of coffee and picked up another sandwich.

—The radio said the city's in one hell of a mess, she went on. —There's been a general riot – did you know? It's still going on. ... But I see you're not very interested.

Ariston stopped chewing and gave her a blank stare.

—Why should I be? Should I care if the city gets burnt to the ground?

—All right, all right. I was only making conversation, she said soothingly. —What do you want to talk about, then?

He started chewing again and considered the question.

—Tell me about this place, he said. —The people who live here. For a start, you. Who are you?

—I'm Anne Ewing, Mr. Mackleford's secretary.

He glanced at her bathrobe.

—Secretary, huh?

—That's right. I'm his very private, confidential secretary.

—I'll bet.

—No, it's not how you think. I live here. Everyone's out, so why shouldn't I go around like this? And Mac's wife lives here too, I hasten to add. Cathy's a witch.

—*Witch*?

—Sort of. Likes to play with people. Very devious. Watch out for her.

—I'll bear that in mind, he said. —Who else lives here?

—No-one. The cook and the maid sleep out. Oh, there's a houseguest just now – the Mechanical Laugh.

—The who?

—Well, that's what I call him. You'll find out why when you meet him. He's Don Fennel, a creep director from the film studio. He's staying with Mac while the two of them work on a project together. ... More coffee? She offered.

He shook his head.

—When are the others due back?

—Why? she asked, pouting mockingly. —Did you have something in mind?

—I'd like to get some more sleep, he said. —Just that. It's been a full day. So if your boss isn't going to be back soon I'll clear off.

—Clear off? Where?

—Dunno. Find somewhere to sleep. A hotel.

—You won't. There's no hotel around here or anywhere else you could sleep.

—I can sleep anywhere. On the beach.

—Don't be ridiculous. You must stay here. I'm sure that's what Mac must have intended. He'd be just furious if I let you escape.

She stood up, folding her bathrobe around her.

—Well, as you'd like to rest before Mac comes back ...

Not looking at her, not stirring, Ariston sat, finishing the last sandwich.

—When's he due back?

—Not for a while. A good while. They went into the city, so the rioting will hold them up. They might not even get back till morning.

Turning, she started to walk towards the stairs.

—Come.

Slapping crumbs off his hands, he rose, followed her up the stairs to the landing. She led the way along a corridor, stopped at a door and opened it.

—You can have this room, she told him, switching on the light. —The bathroom's through there.

—Thanks, he mumbled as he walked in.

She came in behind him and switched off the light. He turned, frowning. Moving in close, she wound her arms around his neck and kissed him. A slow, deep kiss. When it was over he gently but firmly freed himself, took a step back.

—I said I'd like to get some rest. And anyway, I'm pretty sure you've had yours already this evening.

She smiled.

—Come now, drummer boy. I'm curious. You've a reputation to live up to.

She took a step back, undid her robe and let it fall to the floor.

—Come on now, drummer boy. ...

Her pale-gold body glowed in the semi-darkness. Ariston smiled tiredly and reached out. With one fingertip he touched her right breast, pressing the nipple lightly. His finger circled the nipple meditatively, spiraled down and around the breast, returned to caress the nipple and curved away again. It began to sketch on her skin. From her right breast it skimmed across to the other, fondled it, retreated. While they stood there almost at arm's length, she naked, he fully dressed, he repeated the involuted figure-of-eight filigree again and again. His smile was drowsy now. He seemed to be dreaming, hardly to see her.

His fingers drifted casually across her torso, the palm of his hand occasionally brushing her firm, soft belly. She sighed, swaying slightly from side to side, as his finger slid down to her cunt and gently pushed in between the moist lips, probing, coaxing.

—Stop teasing me. ...

She went down on her knees, pulling his fly open and shoving her hand in.

—You won't be able to get it out like that, Ariston told her, unbuckling his belt.

She dragged down his jeans and took hold of his prick with both hands.

—It's marvelous, she murmured, smiling up at him. —I'd like to choke to death on it.

She bit the tip playfully, pouted at it, kissed and held it against her cheek. Eyes closed, a look of blissful innocence on her face, she opened her mouth and took in as much as she could. Slowly she drew her head up, sucking hard, then brought it down, jacking him with her hands at the same time. Ariston grabbed a fistful of her blonde hair and jerked her back. She sprawled on the floor.

—That'll do with that, he said.

She helped him off with his boots and jeans, then he shoved her down and was inside her, pushing up as far as she could take it. He fucked her with an almost mechanical ferocity, pinning her down by the shoulders and driving at her with smooth piston thrusts. He couldn't have told from her moans and cries if she was in pleasure or pain, but he wasn't bothered either way. He hardly heard her. He thought, felt, sensed nothing except his cock driving into her. It didn't stop at her first climax. Her body wanted to relax, if only for a minute, but it didn't get the chance. He thrust relentlessly in and in at her. At her second orgasm she thought she was going out of her mind. She clawed at him, bit him. It made no impression, and she hugged him close now, laughing, sobbing, imagining herself lying in a field and a white bull snorting and slavering over her. As if reading her mind, Ariston turned her over and mounted her from behind. ...

After her third orgasm he picked her up and carried her to the bed. She lay there loosely, her legs limp, boneless. Ariston peeled off the rest of his clothes, pushed her damp thighs apart and drove in at her again. She moaned and kissed his eyes, his nose, his lips, his cheeks, kissed him and moaned and kissed him again.

After her fourth orgasm she lay quite still, staring up at him, one arm hanging over the side of the narrow bed. Her legs were feeling the strain.

—Aren't you ever going to finish? she asked, wonder in her voice.

He said nothing, just drove in and in on her.

After her fifth orgasm. ...

After her sixth orgasm. ...

After her seventh. ...

After her eighth. ...

After her ninth orgasm a light swept across the ceiling and there was the sound of an approaching car.

—It's them! she told him.

He paid no attention.

—It's *them*! she repeated, her voice rising in alarm. —They've come back. Stop. Stop – *stop*, won't you! ...

He didn't seem to hear. From somewhere she found the strength to pummel his back with her fists.

—Stop! she pleaded, panic-stricken. —Please ... *please*! ...

She tried to twist from under him. He held on and they toppled together off the bed and thumped onto the floor. Lightning exploded in Ariston's brain. He shot his juice into her in three spasms. As he relaxed she managed to roll free of him. She scrambled to her feet and ran out of the room, dragging on her bathrobe as she went.

Ariston lay on the floor, the tired, drowsy smile back on his lips. He heard the car draw up, its doors slam, then voices downstairs. He stood up and walked across to the bathroom.

When he came downstairs there were four people sitting about in the living-area. A tall, heavy, middle-aged man rose and came up to him. He thrust out his hand.

—So there you are. Welcome. I'm Austin Mackleford, he announced. —Sorry I couldn't be here sooner. The city's in absolute chaos – but then you know all about that, I suppose. Glad to see you're in one piece. That's the main thing, eh?

He seized Ariston's hand in a fiercesome grip, put an arm round his shoulders and brought him to the others.

—You've already met my wife, of course, Mackleford said, indicating the woman in the bathrobe. —Cathy decided to stay at home tonight. Very wise, as it turned out.

Ariston thought he had misunderstood him.

—Your wife? ... No, I haven't. ... I mean, your secretary. ...

—My secretary ... ?

Mackleford, not quite taking in Ariston's confusion or passing over it, had turned to a small dark girl wearing glasses.

—This is my secretary – Anne Ewing – and a very efficient one she is too, he added, smiling benignly at her before waving a hand towards the last member of the group. —And this is Don Fennel.

Fennel, an aged young man, was thin. Everything about him was thin: the lips and nose of his narrow face, the bony hands lying on the arms of his chair, even the vaguely fair hair retreating from his lined forehead. His only response to the introduction was to blink his bird-bright eyes two or three times before he switched his gaze from Ariston to the woman in the bathrobe.

Ariston's gaze too shifted to her.

—Now, said Mackleford, smiling amiably at Ariston, how about a drink? Whisky?

Ariston was frowning questioningly at the woman Mackleford had introduced as his wife. She met his frown with composure, almost blankly, her face expressionless but for a tiny betraying lift of amused mockery at one corner of her mouth. Fennel was watching both of them, his alert, suspicious eyes flicking back and forth from one face to the other. He saw clearly something was going on between the two. Or had gone on. Suddenly he reacted. Clapping his hands together in delighted realization, he threw back his head and his mouth, opening wide, released a high-pitched staccato braying.

Cathy smiled at Ariston.

—The Mechanical Laugh, she said. —Right?

THERE WERE various reports, rumors and theories about what had occurred at the sports stadium on the night of Satiety Incorporated's performance. Because of the hysteria, the panic and the failure of the stadium's electrical system no-one, not even the journalists and photographers sent by the media to cover the event, really knew what actually happened. It was argued by some that the whole group had escaped by helicopter. Others claimed that the rescue bid had come too late and that all had perished. Yet others opined that Satiety Incorporated had never even entered the stadium: it was five stand-ins who had or had not been slaughtered, while the real Satiety Incorporated were alive and well and living in hiding and would remain so till it was safe to emerge. In a television discussion between an anthropologist and a psychiatrist, the former insisted that the boys had been ingested by their fans and that this fate could be understood only as a sacramental killing and eating of the tribal god, that their flesh and blood, seen as the staff of life and the sacred wine, had been supped as fertility guarantees, blah, blah, blah ... while the latter ingeniously contested that Satiety Incorporated had never in fact existed but had been a mass hallucination which had terminated in a psychic implosion. Officially, Malk, Sonny, Bobs, Toots and Ariston were listed as missing persons.

Casualties among the fans at the stadium, excluding those suffocated to death in collapsed tunnels, consisted of twenty-six dead by crushing and trampling and one by electrocution (which was why the lights blew). Two hundred and thirty-nine were seriously injured (mostly concussion cases). Forty-four policemen were also injured and one bodyguard had an eye gouged out. These figures were only a gentle suggestion of the havoc to come.

A time of rioting followed the show. After leaving the stadium the frenzied fans rampaged through the neighboring streets smashing shop windows, overturning and setting fire to parked cars and otherwise releasing their boiling emotions in a destructive and anti-social manner, and were spontaneously joined in this orgy of violence first by the layabouts from nearby amusement arcades, then by herds of doll people (always easily influenced), next by large gangs of motorcycle creeps, and finally by the city's thugs and minor crooks – in fact by anyone who had a chip on his shoulder or just felt like letting off steam by breaking something. Escalation occurred at a wild pace and within a matter of a few hours whole districts of the city fell completely under the control of the rioters.

There had been troubles before, but never like this. Smitt, the chief of police, decided that if he was going to crush this rabble of maniacs he would need some help. He immediately appealed to the city president for the militia to be called in and placed under his control, and his request was promptly granted. His instructions to his men were that order was to be restored as quickly as possible and at any cost. Looters to be shot on sight.

Eye-witnesses have vouched for the relish with which the police and militia gave effect to their orders. During the first few days it almost seemed that they were playing a sort of game, competing between themselves to see how many people they could maim. Rioter or innocent bystander, thug or old woman, doll or lost child – it didn't matter. The streets were to be cleared. A lesson had to be learned and they knew how best to teach it: a rifle butt in the kidneys, a boot ground in the face of the fallen, tear-gas squirted into the eyes to blind and disfigure. Do it, just do it. Get the job done.

The list of the dead and injured grew longer and longer, but oddly enough the lesson wasn't sinking in. Instead of crushing the rioters, the brutal tactics of the police and militia molded the chaotic elements of an unplanned rising into something like an organized and coherent resistance. By the fourth day after the rioting had started it was obvious that the police and militia were not going to have it all their own way. Barricaded behind high lines of ripped-up paving-stones, burnt-out cars, looted furniture, rubbish, and armed with weapons looted from sports shops, the insurrectionists first successfully held the forces of law and order at bay, then routed them.

Smitt was stunned. His views had always been that the public, rioting or non-rioting, were a lot of soft shits and could in no circumstances be a match for his men. And now the president was breathing down his neck and his very job was in jeopardy. He sat at his desk and chewed his fingernails. How had this thing happened? How? And what was the remedy?

Smitt, failing to come up with an answer, was sacked on the seventh day of the riots and his deputy, Gifforth, became chief of police. Gifforth, much more intelligent than his predecessor and endowed with some powers of imagination, had already toured the lines, observed the enemy with a speculative eye and spent a great deal of time in considering the way out. With praiseworthy acumen he had noted that the rioters all had one characteristic in common, a certain melodramatic self-consciousness. They were, it suddenly came to him, all acting out inner dramas of some sort. It may have been that the entertainment fantasies on which they had been raised had affected their brains; that didn't matter. What mattered was that the rioters' drama-lives obviously thrived on the kind of opposition that was being offered by the police and militia. The solution was simple; remove the opposition, change it. Consequently Gifforth's first order on taking office was that the militia should be withdrawn and that the majority of his own force should go home for a well-deserved rest, a course of action which made many consider that he had totally failed to grasp the seriousness of the situation. His next step stunned them. He ordered pop music to be played through the public announcement systems on police vans for the entertainment of those behind the barricades. His third move caused his critics to conclude that his mind had cracked, that he was as ga-ga as the rioters his job was to suppress and remove. On his instructions the remaining police made charge after charge at the barricades armed, not with truncheons and tear-gas, but with bouquets of roses, lilies and poppies, which they tossed across to the rebels while shouting slogans such as "God is Love" and "Peace and Love." They also invited the enemy to change roles: "Now *you* be the cops and *we*'ll be the rebels!" It worked. Those and other playful suggestions of that puncturing ilk were soon seen to have a deflating effect on the morale of the barricaded. A growing listlessness passed through their ranks, and after two days of this treatment the majority of the rioters quite suddenly became completely fed up with the whole farcical business of rebellion and went home. The state of emergency was ended.

Throughout the civic war Ariston lived in secrecy and in comfort in the house on the beach.

THE SUN striking hotly through the window woke Ariston from a deep dreamless sleep. A glance at the clock on the bedside table told him it was far too late to hope for any breakfast. He lay dozing for a while, then threw aside the bedclothes and ambled across to the bathroom. It was only in the shower, as cold water spurted down against his sleep-soft body, that he really woke up. He stood under the cold spray for a minute, then turned the water warm, soaped himself all over and rinsed off with cold again. When he'd toweled and pulled on his jeans he padded downstairs.

There was no-one about, except Martha, the cook, fixing a salad lunch in the kitchen. He cadged a glass of milk and some biscuits from her and wandered back upstairs with them.

The balcony running alongside Ariston's room overlooked the expanse of lawn where after his morning's work Mackleford set up an archery butt and practiced for an hour or so with bow and arrow. Ariston settled into a cane chair and, munching and sipping, watched the toxophilite go through the same series of movements again and again, taking an arrow, nocking it neatly, sighting and drawing, finally loosing the bow. Arrows whistled through the air, hitting the target in the bull's eye or near it every time. Finer aspects of the archer's technique – his use of the Mongolian draw instead of the more usual Mediterranean, for example – were beyond the appreciation of the present audience (who had finished his milk and biscuits and was devoting more attention to sucking his teeth than to the exhibition being given below), but Mackleford's accuracy alone was enough to make his skill obvious. Ariston's eyes followed Mackleford as he put the bow down on the white metal table beside him, walked to the butt, pulled out the dozen or so arrows and walked back with them. He began shooting them off again. Ariston lost interest and closed his eyes.

It wasn't long before Mackleford gained another observer. A stooped, shabbily dressed man came round the side of the house and stood silently a few yards behind him.

—Very good, he commented drily as Mackleford sank the tip of his last arrow into the bull's-eye. —Quite remarkable marksman, aren't you?

Mackleford twisted round quickly at the sound of the voice.

—Oh, it's you, Brindsley. Didn't realize anyone was there.

Brindsley nodded.

—Well, you might say I'm not really anyone, he said in his quiet hoarse voice. —Isn't that so, Mackleford?

Mackleford chuckled.

—How are you these days? he asked patronizingly.

—Lousy, Brindsley answered. —Just lousy, as if you cared.

—But I do, I do, Mackleford assured him. —And if things are rough just now I'd be glad to lend you a little something.

—You hypocritical bastard, Brindsley said evenly. —I don't want any of your hand-outs. I want what's mine.

Mackleford brushed the other's words aside with a flick of a hand.

— Not that old tale of woe again! Look, Brindsley, you were perfectly happy with our agreement when you signed it.

—*Happy*! snapped Brindsley. —I was down and out. Either I accepted your offer for the book or I starved.

—There you are, laughed Mackleford. —I saved you from starving — and you act as though I'd done something illegal!

—No, Mackleford, you've done nothing illegal. That's the last thing I'd accuse you of. You took my work, put your own name to it and tricked me out of a small fortune, but it was all perfectly legal.

—I'm glad to hear you say so, smiled Mackleford, turning away. —And now you've had your little whinge I suggest you move off like a good fellow.

Brindsley grabbed him by the arm.

—I'm not leaving here until –

With one large hand Mackleford gave him a casual, dismissive push in the chest that was still powerful enough to send him stumbling backwards and down onto the grass, with the other he laid his bow gently on the garden table.

He turned and looked down calmly and contemptuously at the sprawled figure on the grass.

—Listen, you poor simpleton, he told Brindsley as the other man climbed slowly to his feet, I'm getting a bit tired of you and your persecution mania. I may not have written the load of junk you brought to me but I edited it – more than that – re-wrote your muddled scribbling! I promoted it, filmed it – and that's what made it pay, not your literary genius. Yes, there was a good idea somewhere in that muddle, I give you that. That's what I bought, that's all. I paid you what the mess was worth at the time – if anything, too much – and now you've drunk away the money you come crawling back to see what you can wheedle out of me!

Brindsley's face had become blotched with red.

—I don't want any of *your* money, he said, his voice high, hysterical. —I want *my* money – and I want to see *my* name on the title page of *my* book. *MY* book, Mackleford, *MY* book!

He went on shouting, his arms raised, fists clenched in impotent threat.

Up till now Ariston had been vaguely and unconcernedly aware of the voices of the two men, but when Brindsley's voice rose he opened his eyes and paid attention to what was happening. He watched as Mackleford responded to Brindsley's continuing rant by seizing hold of him and shoving him forcefully in the direction of the driveway.

—You're lower than a plagiarist, Mackleford, you bastard. You're –

Mackleford gave him another powerful push.

—Go on, get off my property!

Brindsley steadied himself, then suddenly ran forward and threw himself bodily at Mackleford, his fingers seizing and digging into his fleshy throat. The pair, unbalanced, fell struggling to the ground, began rolling backwards and forwards on the lawn. The fight didn't last long. Mackleford was fifteen years older than his opponent but in much better condition. He quickly broke the younger man's grip, pinned him down with his knee and began to smash his fists into his face.

When his rage had passed he dragged the loser to his feet.

—Don't you ever come back here, Brindsley, he panted. —If you show your demented face here again I'll plug an arrow into it!

Up on the balcony Ariston watched the stranger retreat unsteadily and disappear from view.

ARISTON, SUPPORTING himself on hands and knees, moved rhythmically in and out of Cathy. He was taking it slow and easy. Cathy's long legs were hooked over his shoulders – it was the position she found combined maximum pleasure with minimum exhaustion during their marathon sessions together – and her hands were folded behind her head. A lit cigarette was between her lips.

—You know, Ariston, she mumbled, that potion or whatever it is you give old Mac for his droop is certainly doing things for him. Last night, for example, he managed to get it up again. Quite randy, he was.

Ariston had his eyes shut. He nodded.

—And that's not all, Cathy went on. —He's actually got himself a mistress. Would you believe it? Some red-headed bitch. He had the nerve to boast about her to me.

Ariston smiled. Cathy took the cigarette out of her mouth.

—Why the knowing smile? You don't think I'm jealous, do you? she snorted. —I can't stand him, can't stand being touched by him. But I'm worried.

—About him?

—About *me*, stupid.

He said nothing.

She reached up and tugged a strand of hair that had fallen over his forehead.

—Why don't you look at me when I'm talking to you? she complained.

Ariston's eyes opened. Cathy smiled her appreciation and started to twist the lock of hair round her finger, letting it spring loose and re-winding it again and again as she talked.

—He's a sly old bastard, she remarked of her spouse.

—Not like you, Ariston muttered.

She frowned and pulled at the strand of hair quite hard. Ariston knocked her hand away.

—He's up to something, Cathy confided. —I can see it in his eyes. I'm sure he's aiming to ditch me — and when Mac ditches a wife he leaves her with sweet nothing. He has this bunch of crooked lawyers working for him, divorce specialists — a girl just doesn't stand a chance.

—You could find yourself some lawyers too.

—It wouldn't work. He has too much against me.

—Ah.

Ariston nodded, smiled, closed his eyes.

—Listen, will you! Cathy urged.

—I'm listening.

Cathy scowled. She brooded for a minute before continuing.

—Well, she said matter-of-factly, before he gets rid of me I thought it would be a good idea to get rid of him. Not to put too fine a point on it, I suggest we bump him off.

—Uhuh, he grunted.

—*Uhuh*! Is that all you can say? *Uhuh*?

—What d'you want me to say?

She blinked up at him. What kind of an idiot was he? All his brains were in his prick.

—I want you to tell me what you think of the idea! she exploded.

Ariston pondered as he rode up and down, in and out.

—You're drying up inside, he told her. —Where's the lube?

Cathy stretched out to the bedside table and handed Ariston a squashed tube of vaginal cream. He paused briefly to lubricate her.

—Well? she asked as he started into action again.

—Well what?

Exasperated, she dragged heavily on her cigarette and fiercely blew out smoke. She held up the cigarette to him.

—I can't reach the ashtray.

He took the stub and crushed it out. Cathy began to pet his face, stroking his cheeks and smoothing his hair. She spoke as to a little child.

—I want you to get rid of him for me just as you got rid of that cigarette, she murmured. —He's used up, finished. I want rid of him. Will you do it for me ... for *us*?

Ariston laughed.

—What's so funny? Cathy wanted to know. —You don't believe I mean it, do you?

—Oh, yes I do.

—Then what's your answer?

—No.

She stopped petting him.

—You won't do it? Why not? With him out of the way, if we had his money ... You're scared. That's it, isn't it? You haven't the guts to kill him.

Ariston ignored her.

—I've seen it before, he smiled.

—What? What're you talking about?

—On television. In movies. Lots of times. It's always the same, isn't it?

—I always thought you were a bit simple, Ariston. Now I know it. You're rambling.

—Murder films, he explained. —Rich husband, young wife, lover. Lover kills husband for wife and money. Wife turns lover over to the cops and scoots off with the loot. Not very original, are you?

—But it won't be like that. I couldn't hand you over to the police, Ariston. I couldn't do without you. I just couldn't.

—Couldn't you?

—No.

—Not ever? Never get tired of me?

—*Never*.

—I'd like to believe that.

Ariston suddenly speeded up a little. Cathy gasped.

—I promise you it wouldn't be like on television or in the movies, she protested. —You're the most marvelous lover, the most marvelous ever. I could never let you go. ...

—That's what you say now, he muttered, and he sank into her faster, harder.

—Ariston, you're going too deep – you're hurting. ...

He gripped her shoulders and thrust in at her.

—Ariston, please. ... I'm tired. I can't ...

For ten, twenty, thirty minutes more he held her to their coupling, until she was oily with sweat and there was a look of complete exhaustion on her face.

—Ariston, she begged, you've got to stop now. I can't take any more. Please.

He withdrew, rolled over and lay gazing up at the ceiling. Cathy, moaning with relief, straightened her legs.

—You said you could never let me go, Ariston commented, smiling. —Never. Never get tired of me, you said.

—It's not that, Ariston. It's –

—After you get what you want, he interrupted, you don't want it. Or to put it another way, sex is a *bore*. And when you begin to think like *that* you soon realize that you just might be able to struggle along without me – should you get your hands on Mackleford's loot, that is.

—Ariston, I swear –

—Besides, Mac saved my life. I almost forgot.

—Only so that he could use you, Ariston. Remember that too.

—The answer is no.

He heaved himself to his feet and pulled on his jeans.

—Where're you going? Cathy asked listlessly.

—To my room. Have a shower, then down to the beach for a swim. Coming?

The casual invitation made her stare. I suggest murder and he suggests a swim. Nothing bothers him, nothing gets at him. He really is a child. Or an idiot. Both. *Besides, Mac saved my life. I almost forgot.* He actually said that!

Cathy giggled.

—Ariston, she spluttered, you're the most *innocent* person I've ever known.

MACKLEFORD'S STUDY was a large ground-floor room. Its walls were impressively lined with books (bought in bulk from a dealer who specialized in form rather than content, the binding rather than the bound) and were further ornamented with ancient and modern weapons, a collection of hunting-horns and several oil paintings of the chase. French windows faced the beach, giving a generous view of sea and sky. It was a light and spacious room but its atmosphere, perhaps because of the weaponry, perhaps because of the shelves of somber books, was at odds with the sunshine streaming in and the open view.

Mackleford sat with his broad hands resting on the desk-blotter and gazed out of the window. He could see Ariston and Cathy on the beach. They had just come out of the water and, laughing and talking, were plodding up through the sand to the house. The morning's mail had been dealt with; he had dictated the necessary replies and a few other letters to Anne, and she had left him some minutes ago to type them. He should get on with the new script now. God knows he was far enough behind with it. Finish one thing and start on the next straightaway, that was how he'd always worked. Till recently. Never letting time slip by wasted, that's how he'd got where he was. And so ...

But instead of setting to work like the earnest hack he was – or used to be – Mackleford continued to sit motionless as death. Only his slightly bulbous eyes moved as he watched the dripping pair trudge nearer, and when Ariston and Cathy passed out of his field of vision his eyes too became quite still, staring straight ahead over the sea, focused on nothing.

Of course the bastard was having it off with Cathy – just as all the others had done. But that didn't matter; that was something he had foreseen when he first thought of bringing the little squirt here. He was the last of a long line. One more, what difference did it make? She'd had about a hundred to date. So he could stay here till he felt like leaving and do what the hell he wanted with Cathy just as long as he kept up the supply of that stuff, whatever it was. He didn't like to think what went into that witch's brew. Tasted a bit like yoghurt – horsepiss flavor! Whatever it was it had worked, made a man of him again! He'd proved that last night to his satisfaction – and hers! She'd been surprised, all right. Yes. He'd tried everything before this, spent a pile, and this was the only remedy he'd found. Whatever it was.

Mackleford turned his blind gaze away from the seascape. He picked up the folder in front of him, opened it and began to leaf through the typescript inside. He made a note here and there, changed a few lines of dialogue; but he knew he was only fiddling about. It was so difficult to concentrate these days. After a while he started to doodle in the margins. Gradually the traceries became more and more intricate and suggestive.

There was a gentle knock on the door. That would be Anne with the letters to be signed. He flipped over a page to hide the doodles.

—Come in, he called.

He kept his head down, so that when the door opened Anne's idea of him as the hardworking writer-producer would be maintained. But the door didn't open. Thinking she hadn't heard, he called again, this time more loudly.

—Come in!

Still no-one. He must have made a mistake. Frowning, he tried to fix his attention on the words in front of him.

Damn – there it was again!

Mackleford felt distinctly irritated, but he kept his temper under control and when he spoke his voice was perfectly calm.

—Yes, come in.

He twisted round in his chair and stared at the door.

It showed no intention of opening, no matter how hard he stared. Mackleford stood up and walked over to the door, opened it and glared out into the corridor. There was no-one there.

What was this, some stupid joke? Resisting the temptation to slam the door, Mackleford shut it quietly, and then stood with arms akimbo and waited. When the knock came again he was ready. He snatched the door open and Anne, startled at this lightning reception, let the sheaf of letters she was holding drop from her hand.

The two stared at each other.

—It's you, said Mackleford.

Anne blinked.

—Yes.

They bent to gather up the scattered sheets of paper.

—Did you go back for something? Mackleford asked gruffly.

—What d'you mean?

—Before – when you knocked before – you didn't come in, he explained, straightening up. A rather annoying thing to do. I suppose you forgot a letter and went back for it – was that it?

—I'm sorry, Mr. Mackleford, I don't understand. I've only just this minute finished typing the letters and I brought all of them through right away.

She handed him the letters she'd picked up. Mackleford cleared his throat.

—I see. Well, it doesn't matter.

He returned to his desk with the letters and scrawled his signature across the foot of each.

—Is there anything else you want to go in the post? she asked as she took them from him.

—No, that's everything, I think.

She turned to go.

—Oh, Anne?

She paused.

—Yes?

—I was wondering, did you happen to see anyone in the corridor as you came along just now?

She gazed at him for a moment before answering.

—In the corridor?

—Uh, yes. Someone knocked on the door just before you and I was wondering if ...

—No, I didn't see anyone.

—You're sure?

—Yes, Mr. Mackleford.

It seemed to Mackleford that behind the lenses of her glasses her eyes had an amused look. He avoided her gaze.

—Anyway, it's not important. That's fine, that's fine, he said, starting to close the door.

He stood frowning at the closed door, feeling annoyed with himself for not keeping his mouth shut. There were other possible explanations for that knocking noise, but he had no intention of investigating any further and making a complete fool of himself.

He forced himself to resume work on the scenario and had started sketching out a new scene when – quite clearly – he heard it again. Mackleford jumped to his feet, rushed to the door and wrenched it open.

Once more the corridor was deserted. He walked along to Anne's office. It was empty. Further along was the doorway of the kitchen. Martha was humming cheerily as she worked. She turned from the dishwasher with a pile of crockery and almost dropped it as she found herself confronted by the red-faced figure of Mackleford. He glared at her, then, dismissing her from the list of suspects, grunted and continued on to the living-area.

He didn't usually drink in the morning, but his mornings weren't usually like this one. He poured himself a stiff whisky and gulped it down. As he glanced out of the window he saw the butt out on the lawn and he considered going out for some practice to ease his nerves.

He had to go back to the study for a bow, and as soon as he entered the room he saw what had happened. The upturned bottle of ink. The scenario script flooded, ruined. Cursing softly, he righted the bottle, pulled out his handkerchief and mopped at the pool of ink with it. Had he knocked over the ink when he dashed for the door? Surely he'd have noticed at the time?

He looked up and saw Anne standing in the doorway.

—I ... It seems I've been rather clumsy, he muttered. —This means extra work for you, I'm afraid.

She came across and lifted the folder, and as she picked it up some of the pages fell open at Mackleford's erotic doodles. She looked up at him coolly.

—I'll get it re-typed right away, Mr. Mackleford, she murmured.

—Fine, fine, he said, and cleared his throat. —Thank you.

When he was alone he sat down and put his head in his hands. He felt foolish, fuddled, depressed. Then – this time he was half expecting it – he heard the noise again. It was lighter now, more of a tapping. A sharp, staccato here-I-am. Yes, that's how it seemed – as if it was deliberately and impatiently rapping for his attention!

And it wasn't over by the door now. It was closer, much closer.

A most unpleasant chill crept over Mackleford's back. Sweat beaded his brow. *The noise was coming from his desk.* He widened the spaces between his fingers and peered through.

But of course there was no-one. And of course there was nothing. He scanned the various objects on the desk, then wearily closed his eyes, and instantly –

Rat-a-tat! Rat-a-tat!

With a sweep of his arm Mackleford cleared papers, files, manuscripts onto the floor.

Rat-a-tat-tat-tat-a-tat-tat-tat-a–

The tapping was faster now, harder. Where was it, *where was it*? Mackleford was feverishly pushing everything off the desk.

Rat-a-tat-tat-tat-a-tat-tat-tat-a–

As Mackleford reached for the pile of books at the far right corner of the desk the noise accelerated to a continuous, excited rataplan. He hesitated, then slowly lifted the nearest books away.

He neither believed nor disbelieved what he saw. He simply stared and stared. His mind had stood still – and the hand, the thin poised hand that lay closeted among the books, it too was still now, the yellowish nails no longer rapping the desk.

Neither moved. And the hand seemed somehow to be staring back. Then Mackleford shut his eyes tight. He shook his head from side to side as though trying to throw off the horrible image in his mind, and when he looked again the hand had disappeared.

Suddenly he threw back his head and laughed. The answer had come to him in a flash – it was that muck that little shit Ariston was feeding him. It was affecting his mind, hallucinating him – of course, that *had* to be the explanation!

JUST AS originally Mackleford had been intrigued by the rumors of Ariston's fantastic potency – an interest in which had made him see to it that Ariston survived the götterdämmerung of Satiety Incorporated – so, when he discovered from his newly acquired houseguest the existence of an aphrodisiac, an aphrodisiac that *worked*, he became equally interested in the source and ingredients of the restorative. As long as he depended on Ariston for future supplies of the mixture he was a worried man, for he knew that only when he could get or make the stuff for himself would the continuation of his regenerated sexual ability be guaranteed. Besides, there were distinct commercial possibilities. However, neither his attempts to bribe or coax the required information out of Ariston, nor his attempts to have him followed when he went into the city for a fresh supply, had met with any success to date.

With the onset of side effects Mackleford became even more anxious about what went into the aphrodisiac. Attacking the problem from another angle, he sent away a sample of the porridgy muck for analysis and impatiently awaited the results. Meanwhile, torn on the horn between being hallucinated and being impotent, he chose the former. He had fully experienced the all too bitter humiliations of the latter, and stoically accepted that until an improved formula was available he would just have to live with such optical and auditory delusions as presented themselves.

The hand appeared quite often. Sometimes it was there when he was working in his study, sometimes when he was in his bedroom getting ready to go to sleep. Once, when he woke in the morning, there was the hand sleeping (as it were) on his pillow, just a few inches from his face.

It wouldn't be inaccurate to say that a certain sense of companionship developed on Mackleford's part, a feeling encouraged by the fact that these visitations took place only when he was alone. In fact, he began to consider the thing almost as a pet – an undeniably ghastly-looking one, to be sure, but people have chosen ghastlier and been very fond of them. Thus, after an initial nervy phase had been endured (the hand soon dropped the annoying habit of rapping its nails and tapping at doors) it was quite without concern that Mackleford observed the manifestations of this disembodied human paw. Perhaps he would glance up from the re-typed scenario and see the hand scuttling busily across the floor (it had a rather amusing self-preoccupied air about it at such times); he simply continued with his work. Perhaps it would make a bit of a nuisance of itself by switching off the lights when he was undressing (trying to make things spooky!); Mackleford remained placid, just switched on the lights again. Of course, now and then it still managed to give him a fright; for example, the time when it dropped from the top of a bookcase onto his head; on another occasion it crawled up his trousers-leg and gave him a very bad moment. These happenings, however, were little more than games. They occurred during what might be called the honeymoon phase of their relationship.

All honeymoons must come to an end. About a fortnight after the first appearance of the hand Mackleford came back from town, where he had been proving his dearly bought potency to his lively little red-head, and found a police car parked in his driveway. Inside the house he met a plain-clothes man and a uniformed sergeant talking to Martha in the hall. The man in plain clothes introduced himself as Detective Gowan.

–Afraid you've had an uninvited guest this afternoon, sir, he explained to Mackleford.

–What – a burglar?

–Well, that's just it, said Gowan. –There's been quite a lot of damage, but we don't know yet if anything's been stolen. Perhaps you could check up on that now?

–It's one of them hooligans from the city, complained Martha. –Nothing better to do with their time than go around smashing things.

It gave me quite a turn, I can tell you, Mr. Mackleford, when I came back from my afternoon off and saw what had happened.

Grumbling to herself, she turned and retreated to her kitchen.

—OK, so where's the damage? Mackleford asked.

Gowan led the way to the study.

—This is the only room that's been touched, he said as they entered. —But it's been given a real going-over.

Mackleford had halted in the doorway and was standing gazing in stupefaction at the shambles there in front of him. Hundreds of his books, their pages torn and crumpled, lay strewn across the floor. It looked as though every breakable thing had been broken. Two of the oil paintings had been slashed. Mackleford picked his way through the debris to his desk. The contents of the drawers had been tipped out and ink-spattered typescript pages were scattered all around. It was the ink stains, reminding him of the very first appearance of the hand, that made him realize what must have happened.

—Notice if there's anything at all missing? Gowan asked.

Mackleford slowly shook his head, but not as an answer to Gowan's question. He heard Gowan's voice but the words did not register on his stunned mind.

—I didn't think you would, continued Gowan, picking up a silver table-lighter and placing it carefully on the desk. —There are plenty of pickings lying about for anyone interested in that sort of thing. But you'd better take a look in the safe, sir.

Mackleford was still staring at his ruined typescripts, his mind still in a haze.

—What?

—Your safe, Gowan repeated. —When we examined the room earlier we saw you have a wallsafe behind that picture over there. It doesn't appear to have been tampered with but you'd better make sure.

—Yes, of course, Mackleford muttered.

He took out his keys and opened the safe, went through the motions of checking what was in it, then told Gowan nothing had been taken. Gowan nodded.

—All right, so we can rule out robbery as the motive. Of course if you discover later that something's been stolen you'll let us know at once?

Mackleford, losing self-control, flared up.

—There's been nothing stolen! he snapped. —I know what happened!

Gowan raised his eyebrows.

—You *know*?

Mackleford faltered, took a grip, realizing how idiotic he was being. If he as much as mentioned the hand to the police or anyone else he would … He didn't like to think what would happen to him. He'd be finished, that was for sure.

—Well, yes, he said, floundering for an explanation. —I mean, it's obvious, isn't it?

—What's obvious, sir?

Mackleford was stuck. Gowan was looking at him blandly, waiting for an answer. Then he remembered what Martha had said in the hall.

—It was just some vandal, he gabbled at Gowan, waving a hand dismissively in the air. —Don't you see? Some vicious lout. That's all. It must have been. God knows, there are enough of them around – the city's full of them!

A bored look crossed Gowan's face.

—My men went over the whole house before you got here, Gowan explained patiently, and there's no sign of a forced entry. A yob would simply have smashed a pane of glass to get in, but whoever did this seems to have had a key or to have been smart with locks. And he was familiar enough with the household routine to know when the servants wouldn't be here.

—You mean someone's been planning this? asked Mackleford, not believing a word of it but glad to change the direction of the conversation. —Someone's been watching the house?

—Either that or it was someone who knew the house from the inside. Tell me, Mr. Mackleford, who is there who might have held a grudge against you?

—A grudge? I don't see … you mean …

Gowan smiled wryly.

—When you've been in this job a while you're never surprised what some people will do out of spite. And frankly, this mess looks very like a spite job to me. You may find it difficult to ...

But once again Mackleford was only vaguely aware of what was being said, once again his thoughts had slipped out of focus. He raised a hand to his forehead. He couldn't handle this ... he needed ... He sank onto a chair.

One thought was clear enough. He had to get rid of the police as quickly as possible. Peace and quiet – some peace and quiet was what he craved for right now. A little time to let his head clear. Peace and quiet and a little time to himself, then he'd be able to take in what was going on, what was happening to him. He was in no condition at the moment to discuss this supposed break-in with Gowan. Anyway, he already *knew* what had happened. Didn't he? Yes. ... Well, no. ... That was just what he had to get straight. ...

Mackleford's weakened reason tried to assert itself. The hand was a hallucination, wasn't it? So, how could it have created this havoc? This was something real. But then again, how did a hallucination manage to switch off lights or to fall onto your head or to do all the other things it had been doing? Perhaps it was he who had torn the books and broken everything. Split personality. Or perhaps everything was a hallucination. Now *there* was logic for you. On that premise you could explain it all. The tappings, the lights going off, the ruined books and typescripts, the police themselves – all, all were hallucinations. Life a great passing parade of mocking hallucinations, nothing, nothing, really real –

—Mr. Mackleford ... Mr. Mackleford!

—Uh ... what?

Someone was shaking him by the shoulder. Gowan was bending over him with a glass in his hand.

—You'd better drink this, sir. You blacked out.

Mackleford gulped in a mouthful of brandy and immediately started coughing.

—Just take it easy, sir, Gowan soothed. —It sometimes affects people like this. Gives them a bit of a shock, you know, coming home to find the place has been wrecked, but it doesn't always show right away. Delayed reaction, sort of thing.

—Yes. Yes, that's right. Thank you, Mackleford said, handing back the glass. —I'll be fine now.

How to get rid of the police? All at once the answer was obvious. Brindsley. Supply Gowan with what looked like the beginnings of a solution. That would give him something to work on and get him out of the house.

—Detective Gowan, Thinking about what you said, it occurred to me ...

—Yes? Gowan prompted.

—Well, you asked me who might have had a grudge against me, and I suddenly remembered ...

Again Mackleford paused, hesitant. Gowan waited patiently.

—Maybe I shouldn't tell you about him, Mackleford continued. —I mean, he's probably got nothing to do with this, after all.

—Probably not. But if we find he's in the clear there's no harm done, is there?

Mackleford acknowledged the point with a nod.

—There was a fellow called on me here not so long ago, he began. —Brindsley's his name. He'd been a couple of times before, as a matter of fact, but the last time he became quite nasty. Once – a while back – we'd had a misunderstanding over a business arrangement. There was nothing personal in it, no hard feelings, not on my part, at least. I didn't see much of him afterwards and the whole affair was forgotten about as far as I was concerned. Then one day he turned up out of the blue and started raking up the past. Seemed to have a chip on his shoulder, one that was getting bigger and bigger with time. He accused me of all sorts of ridiculous things and finally, as I said, he got quite nasty.

—Did he threaten you in any way?

—Yes, he did. But it was just in the heat of the moment, I'm sure. We had a bit of a scuffle, you see.

—He actually *attacked* you, did he?

—Yes. Then when I warned him off my property he said something about getting even with me. Naturally I didn't take him seriously.

—Maybe you should have, Mr. Mackleford, said Gowan, taking out his notebook. —The guy's name? ... Brindsley?

—Yes, James Brindsley. I'm afraid I don't know where he lives.

—No problem. We'll find him easily enough.

After a few more questions Gowan and the sergeant left. Mackleford chuckled as he shut the front door behind them: he was thinking of the unpleasant surprise poor Brindsley was going to get when the cops turned up showing such a suspicious interest in his doings.

That afternoon Cathy and Ariston had set off on a picnic with Anne and Fennel. Though it was dark now, they still hadn't returned. Martha had already gone home. Mackleford was alone. His chuckles faded, leaving a loose lop-sided smile on his face. He stood aimlessly in the hallway for a minute, than wandered back to the study and began clearing up. But he was too listless to stick to it for long. Leaving the job for the maid to do when she came tomorrow he went upstairs to his bedroom. In spite of the tiredness he felt he somehow doubted whether he was going to sleep well. To ensure a good night's rest he took some strong sleeping pills before undressing and crawling wearily into bed.

He hadn't been long under the covers and was just drifting in the shallows of unconsciousness when the others arrived back. He heard Cathy's voice and Fennel's harsh laugh, but those were the last things he was aware of before he sank gratefully into the black depths. When Cathy came upstairs and into his room and asked him what had happened in the study, she was answered only with heavy breathing and a mucous snort of happy oblivion.

THE NEXT day, Mackleford's last on earth, began early for him. The sleeping draught wore off quickly and he awoke in the wee small hours, that dangerous time when the life force is ebbing in us all, when conscience (if any) stirs, when the cops (a substitute form of conscience) make their nemesis raids, when things supposed to go bump in the night do indeed sometimes go bumpety-bump-bump. To be more precise, it was three-forty and there was no bumpety-bump-bump but instead the tap-tap-tap, the unmistakable tapping of a typewriter. It came from the room directly below. His study.

But who could be typing at this time in the morning? Or was it a typewriter dreaming aloud, an image-tormented machine regurgitating similes and metaphors in its sleep? Mackleford had been tossing to and fro in bed; now, wearily, he gave up the struggle to evade wakefulness, flung back the bedclothes and swung his feet onto the floor. Investigate he must. He was compelled to, in spite of that inner voice that warned him to ignore everything, to let the world of appearances rave on and to try once more to get back to the dreams and the forgetfulness.

Forgetfulness? Dreams? Ha! Death, that was the only forgetfulness. Nor were there any dreams left for him. He was learning that. Only the nightmare remained, the shift and change of fever and despair blending mythopœically in the twilight of sanity. Madness can be anything. A night of total darkness. A glare that burns out the retinas. The full moon. An idea. A person. A smile. A fly buzzing against a window-pane. A hand.

Mackleford had slipped on his dressing-gown and gone out to the landing. Shapes of darkness surrounded him. Fingers scrabbling over the wall, he searched for the light-switch, found it and shuffled to the top of the stairs.

As he reached the hallway the clacking of the typewriter stopped. He paused and waited. The silence of the house sucked at his ears like a vacuum. Still he waited for the noise to start again, but the silence was final. He forced himself to go on.

Turning from the hallway into the corridor, he saw a light shining under the study door. Slowly he approached. His flabby face was expressionless, dewed with sweat. His hand gripped and pushed down the handle and the door swung open.

The room was empty. Mackleford's dull gaze drifted from one end of the study to the other and came to rest on the typewriter. There was a sheet of paper sticking out of it. He crossed the cluttered carpet to the desk, twirled the paper out of the machine and began to read what was on it.

Mackleford cackled. Dirty words. The sheet was covered with them. Bastard. Cunt. Fuck you, shithead. Obscene names. Insults. It was just silly. ... Then his glance fell on a small separate group of words half-way down the page and his cackling was cut short.

YOU STOLE MY BOOK –
NOW YOU ARE PAYING

BRINDSLEY

The words blurred. Brindsley? *Brindsley*? What in hell had that stumblebum to do with this? He'd told the police about him only to get them out of the way – it wasn't possible he'd put them on the right track after all, was it? No, that couldn't be it. There had to be some other explanation. But what? Mackleford screwed the sheet of paper into a ball and let it drop from his hand, then in a sudden hysterical spasm seized the typewriter, raised it above his head and hurled it away from him. It hit the floor with a twanging crash that gave him a lot of satisfaction. He glanced triumphantly around the room and strode out.

Something was burning. He could smell smoke. From upstairs. Mackleford dashed up to the door of his room and threw it open. Thick smoke billowed out into his face, overwhelming him. Coughing and spluttering, he rushed in, stopped, peered about in a watery-eyed attempt to locate the fire. There were no flames. Only smoke, clouds of acrid smoke, densest over by the bed. His streaming eyes screwed up, lips pressed tightly shut, trying to hold his breath, he dashed across the room. Still he could see no flames, but the bed was on fire all right, smoke rising from it thick and fast. How had it happened? He asked himself. He didn't smoke, *he* couldn't have somehow started it accidentally. So what had happened? How? ... Just another mystery, another little turn of the screw – another hallucination? The taunting idea made him laugh, the laugh made him take smoke into his opened mouth, the smoke worse than ever, made his eyes sting and stream as though with acid in them.

He dashed for the window. He had to get fresh air, couldn't stay in this smoke a moment longer. He fumbled at the window, managed to release the catches, heaved the window open.

Ah, fresh air, fresh air!

As he bent down and leaned forward out of the opening to gulp in more fresh air he found himself staring at the hand. It – the damned thing – was right there, close beside him, there on the inner sill of the window he had, or might as well have, so obligingly opened for it, for it was about to crawl out – now *had* crawled out – onto the outer sill and into the fresh air, as though it too needed to get away from the smoke.

– Aaaaaaaaaaa!

With this strangled exclamation of shock, Mackleford, straightening up, jerked away from the hand.

Then he froze, could only gawp mindlessly at the hand as it crawled out onto the outer sill.

Once there, it stopped. The seconds ticked past. The hand remained quite still, as though waiting for Mackleford to try to take the chance being offered him. Go on – catch me if you can, stupid!

Mackleford got the idea. Yes, of course, this was his chance! Slowly he reached out for it, his hand floating nearer, nearer the hand. Patient, waiting, it remained quite still as Mackleford's hand inched cautiously nearer. Then, just as he had summoned up the courage to make a grab for it, was just about to do it, the hand hopped smartly off the sill and parachuted down into the garden below.

Mackleford cursed, bent forward and stuck his head out of the window, peered down into the dimness. Where was it? It must have fallen about ... *there.* ...

But he could see almost nothing, certainly not a sign of the hand. He cursed again.

What was that? He thought he had heard something moving down there in the undergrowth. He strained his ears. ... Just then, however, his concentration was shattered by a different noise – a fierce, loud hissing – behind him. Startled, he drew in his head, whirled round, and promptly received a jet of foam full in the face. Staggering back, a fountain of foam still shooting through the air at him, he slipped on the now wet floor and fell with a bone-shaking thud. Still, as he lay there stunned, confused, foam came pouring onto him.

−Stop it! Mackleford screamed. −STOP!

He clawed froth out of his eyes and staggered to his feet. Standing by the dripping bed, emptied fire-extinguisher cradled in his arms, was Ariston. Then Cathy and Fennel appeared in the doorway. At the sight of the foam-bespattered Mackleford and the guilty-eyed Ariston both burst out laughing.

−Sorry, Mac dear, Cathy gasped, trying to control herself, sorry, but really, you look ... so *funny*!

NOW MORNING had arrived in all its glory. Blue sky was spread out brightly, the sea sparkled but Mackleford was unaware of the beauty being offered him. Indifferent to everything, he sat slumped across his desk. When the phone beside him shrilled he didn't stir.

The instrument rang on insistently. Mackleford straightened up slowly, sighed and picked up the receiver.

—What is it? he grunted.

—I'd like to speak to Mr. Mackleford.

—You are speaking to him. What d'you want?

—Detective Gowan here.

Mackleford nodded, as though Gowan could see him.

—Ah ... yes ... Detective Gowan ...

—Well, Mr. Mackleford, I've only just started working on the break-in at your place but already I've come up with something that's beyond me.

—Really?

—It's like this. I did an immediate records check on the James Brindsley you mentioned. We had him in our files, all right – he'd been arrested a number of times on drunk and disorderly charges – and his fingerprints matched a lot of those we found in your study. In fact, his prints were all over the place. It looked at first as though he was our man.

—What d'you mean, "at first"?

—When I traced Brindsley I discovered it just couldn't have been him.

—You mean he has an alibi?

—An unbreakable one. He's dead.

—Dead?

—Yes, Mr. Mackleford. And he died weeks before your house was broken into.

—Dead? Mackleford repeated. —I don't ... How can he be? What happened to him? An accident?

—Committed suicide. Anyway, what I wanted –

—Wait a minute. Suicide? *Suicide*? Why would he kill himself?

—That's not what concerns us. The point is ...

—No, hold on a minute. You said he committed suicide. I want to know ... I mean, there would have been a coroner's report – right?

—Yeah, there was. It seems he went crazy. He worked nights at some factory and he deliberately shoved his arm into the machinery. His hand was sliced clean off at the wrist and he lost so much blood he died before –

Mackleford held the phone out in front of his face and began yelling at it.

—*Hand*, did you say? The machinery cut off his *hand*? He bawled. —I don't believe a word of it, d'you hear me! And if this is some kind of a trick you'll regret it, Gowan. You won't get away with it. You'll laugh on the other side of your face, I promise you – I'm not without influence, Gowan, as you'll find out!

—Mr. Mackleford, are you all right? ... Mr. Mackleford?

But Mr. Mackleford had slammed down the receiver.

IT WAS shortly after Gowan's telephone call. Mackleford, armed with bow and arrows, was out on the lawn making sure that his aim was as good as ever. It was. Arrow after arrow sped to the bull's-eye. To an observer who knew what was what – one such as yourself, gentle reader – his performance would have been a demonstration that even severe mental deterioration need not necessarily affect visual accuracy and muscular control. That darling morning there were, however, no observers at all. Except for Martha and the maid, who were in the kitchen chatting over a cup of coffee, the house was empty. Anne and Fennel had gone to the studios on business – unknown to Mackleford the project was about to be taken out of his hands – and Cathy and Ariston had quietly disappeared together.

Mackleford practiced on. Then, as he was fetching the arrows from the butt, he saw just what he had been waiting and hoping for. The hand. It was lying on the grass at the very edge of the lawn, partly under a shrub but not in its shade. In fact it seemed to be basking in the sun. Mackleford blinked. For a moment it had looked more like a dead sycamore leaf than a hand. But he wasn't mistaken – it was the hand, all right. Slowly, carefully, he pulled an arrow out of the butt, nocked it and aimed.

The hand was a good distance away. It was a small target, and the angle was bad. If he could get a bit closer it would be so much easier. Mackleford relaxed the bow, crouched down as best he could and crept forward. But the hand was no fool. As he neared, it withdrew warily under the bush. Mackleford gave a shout of fury and rushed forward. He glimpsed the hand scuttling from hiding-place to hiding-place and gave chase through the shrubbery. He was determined to catch the damn thing and put an end to this business. Bellowing, breaking and flattening shrubs in his increasingly frenzied search, he crashed around the garden, a bull elephant on the rampage. Martha and the maid, their attention attracted by the commotion outside, bustled over to the kitchen window and stared out at the antics of their berserk employer. They looked at him, then looked at each other. There was no need to speak. It was understood. Enough was enough. A decent woman could tolerate just so much in a household, even if she was only a servant, even if the wages were good. There's a limit to goings-on. Without a word they took off their aprons, fetched their coats, without putting them on hurried out of the house, climbed into Martha's car parked at the side of the house and drove off.

Meanwhile Mackleford's rampage had come to an end. Exhausted by his exertions, he was standing, hand on his thudding heart, gasping, sucking air into his burning lungs. His quarry, of course, was nowhere to be seen. Neither, he now realized, was his bow. He must have dropped it somewhere. He glanced around, gave himself a few more minutes to recover his breath, then began to retrace his path of destruction.

He found the bow – and the arrow – near the lawn. He picked them up, turned towards the house. Then he froze. The hand. There it was again – and this time he had it. It had tried to climb into a tree, had succeeded in getting about six feet up the trunk: but it was making no more progress, the fleshless fingers were arched, desperate, their long yellow nails, digging into the bark, seemed only just managing to keep it from falling back to the ground. Quickly Mackleford fitted the arrow to the string, drew the bow, took aim.

Yes – he'd go it!

The fingers of the hand splayed out as the arrow hit it square on the back and pinned it to the bark. It jerked in a spasm of agony, another, a last one, then became rigidly still. Bow in hand, flushed with triumph, Mackleford was the very picture of the successful hunter. His eyes gleaming with satisfaction, he hurried over to the tree and gazed at his trophy. His ... finally his.

He wanted to spend a long time examining it right there and then, but he didn't allow himself even to touch it. He knew what he had to do – and the sooner the better. Casting a final exultant glance at the thing skewered to the tree trunk, clutching his beloved bow, he lumbered off towards the house. A few preparations were called for. The hand would be safe as it was for a minute.

The cellar of the house was reached from the hallway by a flight of wooden steps under the main stairway. Still holding the bow, Mackleford switched on the light and clattered down into the damp mustiness. The overhead bulb was covered with dust and cobweb and only half lit the place, but Mackleford knew where to look for what he wanted. He laid the bow aside. A quick rummage through a pile of oddments produced a slim iron rod about eighteen inches long and a two-foot length of strong wire. At a spot directly under the electric light he hammered the rod deep into the earthen floor and to the six or seven inches that were left protruding out of the ground he tied one end of the wire. Rubbing his hands with glee, he trotted back to the garden.

His prize was still there, still impaled on the tree. First he eased the arrow out of the trunk, then out of the hand. The first contact of the dry hard skin against his own made him shudder with mixed revulsion and attraction. He was a man with three hands. The thought made him laugh. But it was risky standing about. Any minute the hand could revive and start struggling to get away. Plenty of time to feast his eyes on it later. First things first.

First things consisted of carrying the hand to the cellar, threading the loose end of the wire through the hole the arrow had made in the palm (there was no sign of bleeding from the wound – not surprising, really) and tying it back in a loop. Having secured his former tormentor, Mackleford felt he could now indulge in the pleasure of a long and detailed scrutiny of it.

It was a hand. Of that there was no possible doubt. Severed two or three inches above the wrist. A clean cut. Uhuh. Nails excessively and unpleasantly long, obviously having continued to grow after the owner's departure. All right. Most of the flesh had wasted away, giving a look of ascetic fanaticism. That's just what it was, a crazy fanatic hellbent on revenge. Vendetta. Well, things hadn't worked out quite that way, had they? Mackleford prodded the hand. It remained entirely inert. He scowled. When was it going to recover? Had he killed it? If he had, that was half the fun gone.

He brought over an empty wooden box, sat down on it and continued his absorbed inspection. About a quarter of an hour later he was highly relieved to see the captive show some signs of revival. It twitched sporadically for a while, did a few preliminary five-finger exercises, then began to crawl tentatively around the iron stake. Around and around it went on its metal leash. Mackleford's fascination now knew no bounds. Not since early boyhood days had any form of animal life captured his imagination and intrigued him like this. Time flowed on, its minutes and hours slipping away unnoticed. He felt he could sit there forever studying that entrancing freak. And thus the last of Mackleford's last morning passed and his last afternoon wore on.

EVENTUALLY MACKLEFORD became aware that some of the others had come back. He could hear footsteps and voices overhead. It sounded like Cathy and Ariston. An idea came to him. He should get a witness. Of course. And who better than Ariston? Eagerly he rose from the box and hurried up out of the cellar. As it happened, Ariston was just passing through the hallway.

—Psst!

Ariston looked round and saw a disheveled and fiercely grinning Mackleford beckoning excitedly from behind the cellar door.

—Down here, he whispered hoarsely. —C'mon! Something to show you. Come ... come!

With repeated imperative gestures Mackleford urged Ariston to come, come quickly, to the door to the cellar. Having lured the reluctant Ariston to the doorway, Mackleford started ahead of him down the stairs, pausing every few steps to turn and gesture yet again.

—Just wait till you see this, he enticed, his eyes wide and wild with wonder and delight, his mouth moist and leering.

Slowly, wonderingly, Ariston followed. He's completely lost it, he thought, but he continued down the stairs. On the bottom step he paused, feeling, oddly, like a diver on a high spring board about to launch himself out into the air and down into a deep descent. He looked around. He'd never been here before. The place reminded him vaguely of the basement where he'd first met Satiety Incorporated and shown them what he could do on the drums. Yeah, he'd really shown them. ... How long ago was that? Very long, it seemed, though it couldn't be, could it? But already so vague it felt like a lifetime away. ...

Mackleford, waving at him from across the cellar, was again demanding his attention. What was the old loony on about? He was pointing at the floor, trying to say something but so excited he was gagging on the words. Ariston walked over, looked down and saw an iron bar sticking out of the ground with a lasso of wire tied to it. He raised his eyes to his host's flushed face. Well then, what was all the fuss about? But Mackleford had become incapable of speech. His mouth hung open, an elastic drool of saliva hung from his nether lip. Ariston shook his head, clapped Mackleford on the shoulder and left him.

Mackleford got down on his knees and examined the wire. How had it happened? To escape in the short time he'd been away – it wasn't possible! The loop wasn't undone – that meant the hand must have pulled the wire through itself! But how could it? And in so short a time? All right, all right, but it was still somewhere in the cellar. Still a prisoner. Mackleford scrambled to his feet and went upstairs, locking the cellar door behind him.

In his study he unhooked a crossbow from the wall and carefully loaded it. He took a torch from a desk drawer and shoved it into his pocket, then returned to the cellar. Arbalest cradled along his right forearm, the torch in his free hand, he began the search. He prowled around, peering into every corner, probing with the torch beam into each shadowy cranny and scrupulously investigating any and every niche that could possibly have provided a hiding-place for the runaway. Then he heard a noise. A distinct scrabbling sound came from the opposite side of the cellar. He whirled round, started to dash over – but suddenly something caught viciously, searingly, at his ankle. Screaming with the pain he crashed to the cellar floor, brought down by ... by what?

He was in agony, he couldn't move, couldn't ... it hurt even more when he tried ... but after a few seconds he forced himself, managed to raise his upper body enough to be able to look down at his ankle.

It was the wire, the loop of wire that had held – failed to hold – the hand. He'd stepped right into it and now it was gripping *his* flesh, had cut into it like a cheese slicer.

With a little whine of pain and self-pity he sank back onto the dirt floor, closed his eyes, lay there, groaning, giving little gasps, another little whine or two.

Only when the shock and the worst of the pain of the surprise attack had passed did he stir. Cautiously he again raised himself up and started to examine his injured ankle. It was bleeding freely. If he'd been wearing socks there would have been some protection; as it was, he had put on only sandals that morning and, with no barrier, the wire had cut in to the bone. He made a tentative attempt to loosen the noose, but the snare had drawn tight and the running knot he'd made had stuck fast and all the fumbling of his trembling fingers succeeded in doing was to make the pain worse.

Mackleford gazed pathetically around. He needed something to cut the wire with. Hanging from a tool-rack on the wall was a pair of pincers; but he was the one on the leash now and the pincers were well out of reach. He turned his attention to the end of the wire that was tied to the stake. It offered no problem. That done, he took the pair of pincers and snipped the wire from his ankle, then, after picking up the crossbow and torch, he limped from the cellar.

Cathy was sitting in the living-area sipping a drink while flipping without much interest through a magazine. She looked up as her bedraggled husband, carrying a loaded crossbow, his leg dripping blood, emerged from the hallway and hobbled away in the direction of his study.

—It seems the servants have run off, she observed drily. —One can hardly blame them.

Mackleford gave no indication of having heard her.

In his study, he put the crossbow and torch on the desk, slumped into a chair and closed his eyes. He was a defeated man, his broken mind aware of nothing except his utter exhaustion and the throbbing of his ankle. He sat completely motionless, and the throbbing grew worse as the ankle began to swell. After a while he told himself he must go to the first-aid box in Anne's office and put something on his wound. He sighed wearily and opened his eyes.

On the desk, beside the crossbow, was the hand. With some difficulty but with dogged determination it was pulling the end of the weapon round so that the bolt pointed straight at Mackleford. He saw the danger but for some reason he couldn't move. He was the rabbit mesmerized by the stoat that is about to seize it. He could only watch.

And now the hand was creeping to the trigger of the crossbow. The spell broke. With a choked shout Mackleford lurched forward. Too late. He managed to grab hold of the crossbow but at the same time the hand pulled the trigger. The bolt caught him square in the middle of the forehead, jolting his head and entire body backwards. His fingers still gripping the crossbow, he slipped sideways from the chair, dropped to the floor, dragging the bow with him.

Ariston, out in the garden during this denouement of Mackleford's life, heard his shout and came over to the French windows. Shielding his eyes from the reflected glare, he peered in and saw his host sprawled on the carpet, the crossbow lying beside him, its bolt embedded in his head. It seemed an odd way to commit suicide. He didn't understand why Mackleford had done it. He understood only that it was time to leave the house on the beach. He turned and walked slowly down through the garden, down across the beach and along the edge of the sea.

Quite soon he was only a dark scarcely moving dot on the long curve of sand where the incoming tide was obligingly washing away his footprints.

OTHERS MIGHT think what they liked, but Jacksall knew that Ariston was still alive. By the itching of his palm he knew it. By the twitching of his nose he knew it – and knew for sure. He never made a mistake where money was concerned. He could smell it hundreds of miles away. That was his gift, his special talent, and it told him in no uncertain terms that somewhere out there in the city was a small fortune, a small runaway goldmine called Ariston, and that he must find him and bring him back. For many days and nights Jacksall had brooded over the gross injustice of Ariston's disappearance and the heartrending loss of income to himself, and while he brooded he gained temporary relief from the itching of his palm by scratching it with a gold coin. And when he wasn't scratching his palm with the gold coin he was rubbing his twitching nose with a red silk handkerchief. But he knew there was only one real cure for the itching and the twitching, he knew he had to find out where the dirty coward was hiding and bring him back into the limelight, even if it was the last thing he did.

With that aim in mind he had hired detectives. He employed them by the dozen. They scoured the city, they hunted high and low, in and out, but their search was without success. Jacksall personally joined in the hunt. He spent his own valuable time wandering the streets, visiting cafes and clubs, rooming-houses and hotels. His other work was neglected. He didn't care. His business went into a rapid decline. Clients switched to other agents. He let them. They didn't matter. Only Ariston mattered, and when he found that goldmine – *his* goldmine – everything would be fine again. He was worth ten times all the others put together, for he was all that remained of Satiety Incorporated. To millions of fans he *was* Satiety Incorporated. Hadn't the band become even more of a phenomenon since its destruction? Wasn't it even more popular dead than alive? It had become a legend. Song sales had zoomed. The merchandising possibilities were fantastic. With Ariston alive, the sole survivor, the sky was the limit. Jacksall itched and twitched uncontrollably at the thought of all that money. Ariston wasn't just a goldmine, or two goldmines; he was a mountain of gold. Oh, how he needed Ariston! For one thing, he needed his signature. Contracts were waiting, like unclaimed inheritances. Money was piling up, his for the taking, yet out of his reach until Ariston put his grubby mark on the dotted line. But he'd be fair with the shit. Sixty-forty – what could be fairer then that? Or seventy-thirty, maybe. No point in being too soft. Even eighty-twenty was quite reasonable. Twenty per cent was plenty for the moron. But where was he? How could he disappear just like that?

The search went on. Jacksall's spies were everywhere. He had a thousand eyes and ears. Sooner or later one of his eyes would see something, one of the ears hear something.

Then, at last, the phone call he had been waiting for. One of his ears had heard something, some very interesting and reliable information. It had reached the ear via a maid who'd just quit her job. She had given an address, the place where she had worked. A certain house on the beach, the home of a certain Mackleford who had a certain houseguest.

Mackleford? *Mackleford*?

When the phone call was over Jacksall sat, still, thoughtful, uneasy, repeating the name under his breath. Mackleford? He had heard that name – but *where*? He tried to place it, couldn't, closed his eyes as though to envisage in his mind where that name belonged. ...

Then his eyes sprang open as he remembered, and he began to tremble and sweat. A movie producer. Horror movies? What did it matter? That shit-house was a producer, so the movies were after his Ariston!

Jacksall dabbed his face with the red silk handkerchief. The idea that he might lose his goldmine terrified him. He must act – and fast. He would sort this out himself. This Mackleford guy was going to find out a thing or two. No-one could mess around with him. What was his was his. Muttering to himself, he strode on his angry little legs from his apartment and took the lift down to the garage. He scrambled into his car, slammed the door, roared up the ramp and into the street and sped off for the house on the beach.

It was quite some way and growing dark when Jacksall reached the area of luxury beach-front residences where Mackleford's house was located. He parked his car some distance away from the house, waited impatiently for the cover of complete darkness before approaching on foot. Caution, above all, caution. He had no plan of action, intended to take things as they came, all he knew was that he was going to get Ariston back even if he had to drag him away by the scruff of the neck. He came to the place, its garden surrounded by a high fence. Not high enough, no problem for a skinny little monkey with not an ounce of fat on him. Up the fence he went, over and down into the garden. He could just make out what looked like some bushes. He crawled forward on all fours and hid among them while he spied out the land.

Only one window was lit on this side of the house. Screened as much as possible by bushes, he crept towards it.

This must be ruining his suit, Jacksall reflected as he pushed his way through the undergrowth on his hands and knees, a suit that had cost a small fortune. And he was making too much noise, maybe giving himself away. He began to have doubts. Had he been too hasty? Did he really know what he was doing? This sort of thing wasn't his line at all, he admitted. You needed training for work like this. Perhaps wiser to have let one of the detectives handle it. But no, no, this was too important. It might be his only chance – a chance he'd waited and waited for. He couldn't trust anyone else to follow up a lead like this. It looked too much like the real thing. Too promising to be left in other hands. Who could you trust these days? People would sell their own mothers into slavery. There had been a terrible decline in business ethics. People took money from both sides. They accepted bribes. It was standard procedure. You never knew where you were with them. He'd learned a long time ago that when you want something done properly you have to do it yourself. An honest man was impossible to find, and if you did happen to find one he was bound to be incredibly stupid. ...

Without realizing it, Jacksall had emerged from the shrubbery and, still on hands and knees, had started to make his way across the lawn, a long slice of which was illuminated by the light falling from the window towards which he was aiming. Absorbed in moral anxieties and indignation, even now, in the middle of the lawn, he was not aware he could be seen by anyone in the house who chanced to glance out in that direction.

His luck held, this far. No-one looked out and saw what might have been taken for a boy in a sharp suit crawling over the lit grass and Jacksall reached the side of the house undetected. There, under the lit window, he crouched, giving himself a minute before his next move. Then, holding his breath, he straightened up and looked in.

He half expected to see Ariston in the very act of signing a catastrophic film contract, with a grinning producer standing beside him gleefully rubbing his hands. Instead he saw a woman undressing. She was very large and very fat.

Jacksall was a small thin man with a weakness for large fat women and this one was enormous. Fascinated, he stared at her acres of flesh. His eyes roved delightedly over her creamy hills and dales. But who was she? According to the maid's information there were two women living in the house: the wife and the secretary. If this was the secretary she might help him just as the maid had. Any employee can be bought.

Jacksall goggled. The employee was quite naked now. She was looking for something, moving about the room and displaying her huge arse and bulging thighs to his eager gaze. Then the woman turned round. She saw a strange face peering at her through the window. She caught her breath. It was one of those weirdies she'd read about. A voyeur. She screamed, reached for something to cover her nakedness. She screamed again and hubby came roaring through. Wordless, she pointed to the window. The face was still there, still goggling. Then it disappeared. She enjoyed another good scream, then began to wrap her immense form in her dressing-gown while hubby thundered out of the back door after the weirdie.

Hubby caught the weirdie by the seat of the pants just as he was climbing over the garden fence. Hubby was even more enormous than his wife. His thick arms bulged with muscle. He hoisted the weirdie off the fence, hurled him onto the ground and proceeded to kick and punch the hell out of him. The weirdie begged and pleaded, babbling out some story about how he had been looking for a business associate, about how there had been a mistake with the address. Hubby wasn't impressed. He wasn't listening. A man must protect his wife from freaks and weirdies. Some people had to be taught a lesson; otherwise they'd never give up their nasty little ways, would they? And it wasn't every day you got the chance to beat someone to a pulp all quite legally, or almost. He didn't need to bother with the police. He knew how to deal with this type. This weirdie was so small and light he could easily hold him up in the air with one hand while punching him with the other. His fist thudded into the weirdie's flesh. Not an inch must escape treatment. He pounded away until the body became like putty in his hands. He kneaded and molded it between his thick fingers, gripped it fiercely by the throat and shook it till the tongue hung out of its mouth, bounced it on the ground and stomped on its face. It was a long time since he'd enjoyed himself so much. When he'd finished with it he tossed it over the fence and marched into the house.

Somehow Jacksall had retained consciousness, somehow, after some time, he managed to stir, to start to drag himself away and to his car. There was a flask of whisky in the glove compartment. He fumbled for it and took a swig, then eased himself into the driver's seat and started the engine. As he drove the road blurred and shifted before his puffed and closing eyes. Sheer determination kept him going. It was a matter of principle. A matter of an itching palm and a twitching nose. So he'd been beat up. They could beat him up as often as they wanted. He'd never give up. Ariston was his. The wrong house. In the dark anyone could have made a mistake like that. He would not be put off, would never abandon his client. He was a man of principle.

Somehow the man of principle reached his apartment. He staggered in and collapsed.

THE AIR was sweet. Never before had he breathed such balmy freshness. A cool breeze riffled the leaves, making the sound of shy whispering. Ariston paused, the better to enjoy his enjoyment. He gazed admiringly at the trees that surrounded him, so tall and straight. Their quiet dignity impressed him deeply. Like guardsmen they stood, the protectors of silence and solitude. Ariston gave a sigh of pleasure. To be alone was to be happy, to be away from human beings a delightful holiday. But the holiday must never end. He would never go back to the city. He would live here in the forest with no company other than that of the trees and animals, free of the human plague that had contaminated him all his life.

He started forward again, touching the trunks as he passed them and letting the low-hanging leaves stroke his face and hair. The thought that all this beauty would probably end up as packing-cases, floorboards, matches and toothpicks filled him with a sense of shame, the same shame he felt when he saw the frantic terror with which the delicate forest deer fled before him. Sooner or later the city would spread out to here. Where he was now walking would one day be a street of fun palaces and arcades, or else a film studio or souvenir factory. The deer would be imprisoned in a zoo or killed, stuffed and stuck in a museum. Nothing could prevent this. Nothing could hold back the advance of the city. Pondering this, he walked on.

When night came he curled up under a bush and went to sleep. His dreams were strange but pleasant, full of delightful images colored in shades of green. The forest had entered his soul. At dawn he awoke well refreshed and set off on his way again. He was very hungry.

After a while he came to a clearing where water from a spring bubbled into a pool. Gratefully he knelt and drank. The water was deliciously pure, as pure as the forest air, and like the air it seemed to cleanse him as he took it into himself. He drank mouthful after mouthful of the clear water, then as he raised his head he saw, at the opposite side of the pool, a large black bird. It was staring at him fixedly and clasped in its yellow beak was what looked like a nut. Not wanting to frighten the bird, Ariston straightened up very slowly.

He watched as the bird proceeded to strike the nut in a business-like manner against a smooth stone. After a half-dozen tries the shell of the nut shattered, and with sideways flicks of its beak the bird cleared away the fragments and exposed the kernel. Throughout this performance the bird had shown its keen awareness of Ariston's presence by pausing every so often to fix its bright eyes on him; now it gave him a long meaningful stare, picked up the kernel and hopped round the pool towards him. Every couple of feet it paused, cocked its glossy head to one side and gave him another sharp look, a routine which was repeated until the bird was almost within arm's reach. Then it dropped its offering and flew off.

A few moments later another bird appeared with another nut, which it too began to break open. Before the task was finished another bird arrived on the scene, then another. All carried nuts, and the clearing was filled with the sound of clicks and taps as the birds hammered away industriously. Ariston, still kneeling, not moving, watched.

A rustling in the foliage above him caught his attention, but before he had time to glance up something landed on his shoulder. It was yet another bird – big and black like the first one – and in its beak was a ripe red berry. It fluttered from his shoulder to the ground, placed the berry near the kernels – there were several now – and left him.

Nuts and berries of various kinds continued to be delivered to Ariston courtesy of his newly acquired friends. Birds were all around him. Not only birds. Happening to turn his head, he caught sight of two deer, a buck and a doe, standing at the fringe of the clearing watching him curiously with their wide liquid eyes. They had lost their fear somehow, but not their shyness, and when they saw they had been noticed withdrew daintily into the forest. More nuts and berries were added to the two neat piles in front of Ariston. He was so hungry he wanted to start eating at once; his eagerness might have been mistaken for impatience, however, so he restrained himself.

Finally the birds flitted one by one into the surrounding trees and didn't return. He seized a fistful of nuts and crammed them into his mouth. They were tasty but dry and needed a lot of chewing. He washed them down with some water, then picked up more nuts. When he'd eaten all the nuts he helped himself to the berries, and when his simple but satisfying meal was over he stretched out on the mossy ground and relaxed.

As Ariston lay looking up through the branches at the blue sky he experienced a peculiar tingling all over his body, particularly in his hands and feet, accompanied by a dizzy drowsiness. His eyelids drooped. He was drifting into a trance of some sort. The breeze blew, and the leaves above him rippled. Intimations of a happiness impossible in human life reached him. He began to understand about trees. They harmed no-one and nothing. They purified the air. Their lives were entirely innocent. And all the time the tingling sensation was increasing. A strange power was flowing into him. Cosmic forces were at work. Eyes still closed, Ariston slowly stood up. He held his arms out straight in line with his shoulders. Thus poised, he became subject to even stronger cosmic influences. The tingling intensified.

Suddenly he was afraid. He wanted to get away – to run away from this place, from whatever was happening to him. To his horror he found he could no longer move. He was rigid, completely rigid. The tingling was painful now and growing worse every second. It was agony. Then, when it seemed he couldn't bear it any more, the pain stopped. In a moment it had disappeared completely, as if switched off. Slowly the fear melted out of his mind. He was at peace. Minutes passed. Hours. Days, perhaps. Time meant nothing. He felt a squirming at his feet, a tentative wriggling. He was putting down roots. His toes, breaking free of his worn and split shoes, lengthened and sought nourishment from the soil. He was growing, growing. His head was a high as the tops of the trees. The wind caressed his branches. Leaves burgeoned from his bark-encrusted fingertips. ...

OF ALL the gangs of motorcycle creeps the most infamous was the Naughty Nihilists, an amalgam of hell-bent Neanderthals numbering over two hundred members who rode and roared under the leadership of Suchandsuch Smith. (I speak of *the* Suchandsuch Smith, unlucky seventh son of a seventh unlucky son, born under inauspicious signs in the year of the Howling Wolf. Six feet six, with eyes of piercing blue, his blonde hair grown shoulder-length, he was striking enough to have been a movie star – he'd had offers – but had chosen instead the life of a 1200c.c. cowboy.) And now he and his band of merry men came thundering out of the heat-hazed horizon, the bikes beneath them gleaming like beautiful proud steeds, almost seeming conscious of their strength, of having power that could meet any demand.

The Nihilists rode four abreast, keeping in close formation, and their long hair flowed back in the slipstream. Of society's misfits they were the aristocracy. Their filthy, grease-smeared clothing was decorated with occult emblems and weird signs and symbols – the haphazard devices of their heraldry – and on the backs of their leather jerkins, set in chrome studs, were the gang mottoes, *Per Ardua Ad Nihil* or the more straightforward, *Fuck Everything*. They wore beads and bangles, ear-rings and nose-rings, medallions and medals, winged Viking helmets and stolen police caps. To motorists they were a disquieting spectacle, and at the first rear-mirror glimpse of the surreal horde bearing down on them many thought it wiser to pull into the side until the horde had passed.

Now, at a certain point, Suchandsuch gave a signal and the long column swung off the highway and snaked down a twisting side road. TO THE LAKE, said a signpost. Every couple of weeks the Nihilists had a major get-together, a convention-cum-orgy; the last one had developed into a full-pitched battle with the cops – they were becoming singularly obstructive lately for some reason – and the cost in fines and medical fees had been so crushing it had been decided to hold the next one far from the city centre, somewhere a man could relax and have a good time without the law cramping his style.

When the Nihilists arrived at the lakeside five or six families were there enjoying a peaceful few hours in the fresh air. They looked up from their sandwiches, soft drinks and flasks of coffee and gaped as their afternoon idyll was shattered with fierce abruptness. Yelling and whooping, revving their engines, skidding across the grass and toppling gleefully from their machines, the bizarre troupe of motorcyclists streamed into the picnicking site. At first the families were too stunned to move, then mothers started fussing, fathers shouting, children wailing, and soon all had packed and fled and the Nihilists had the place to themselves.

Suchandsuch called them together and quietened them down. There was outstanding business to be dealt with. First was the gang's grave financial situation. The treasurer spoke. His discourse was brief, and consisted simply of a suggestion that funds should be restored by organizing a hold-up, a suggestion that surprised nobody as it was the trusty treasurer's standard remedy for the gang's recurrent financial ailments. Three members were nominated for the job. The treasurer told them to see him about the details after the meeting, and that was that. Several other items of general interest followed. A problem of discipline was last on the agenda. A minor revolt against Suchandsuch's authority had been brewing in the ranks. Suchandsuch met the challenge by inviting the ringleader forward for discussion, belting him a couple of times with a drive-chain and then chucking him into the lake.

The splash marked the end of the meeting. Beer was unloaded from pillions and casual drinking began. Wood was gathered and a bonfire built in readiness for the evening's festivities. A few were energetic enough to race their bikes up and down the dirt path that skirted the lake, but most just sprawled around on the grass and waited for the girls to arrive. One restless group wandered off into the forest to see what was there.

Ariston was there. The clearing where he had planted himself was only fifty yards away. The Nihilists blundered into his sanctuary, stopped and eyed him with interest.

—Hey, look at that guy!

—What's he standin' like that for, huh?

They approached. Ariston, arms outstretched, remained completely immobile.

—He's some kinda nut.

—Nah, he's stoned out of his head, that's what.

—What's he supposed to be doing – flyin'?

—He's a tree, said one more perceptive than the others. —Don't you see, he's a tree!

At the words, another Nihilist laughed and slapped his hands together.

—Don't you see, he's a tree, he began to chant. —Don't you see, he's a tree. Don't you see ...

They all started to chant the sentence, pointing at Ariston and twisting their faces into ludicrous, mocking expressions of surprise and delight. Then they were capering round him, snapping their fingers to the rhythm, clapping their hands, gesturing as they chanted:

—Don't you see, man, he's a tree-man. Don't you see, man, he's a tree-man. Don't you see, man ...

But they were soon bored with this. The chant faded out. They stood in a circle and eyed Ariston critically.

—Funny-lookin' tree, ain't he?

—Yeah, ask him what kinda tree he thinks he is.

A bearded face was pushed up close to Ariston's.

—Excuse me, sir, could you tell me what kind of a tree you happen to be?

No answer. Knuckles rapped on Ariston's head.

—Anyone home?

No answer. Again the knuckles rapped.

—Hey, no-one's home. Ain't that a disappointment?

—Yeah, that's too bad. But he's a find, a definite find.

—Right. We'll take the freak back with us — Such'll wanna have a look at him.

Ariston ignored the voices. Their language wasn't his language. He was no longer a human. He was a tree. The wind among the leaves was what he understood, that and that only. As hands gripped him and hoisted him into the air he kept his eyes closed tight and his body completely rigid.

Bearing him triumphantly on their shoulders, the Nihilists returned to the others. Ariston became the centre of attraction. More wisecracks were made at his expense. He was pinched and slapped. Someone threw a bucket of water over him.

—Hey, don't get him all wet, guffawed one of his finders. —Damp wood don't burn so well.

Suchandsuch, who'd just pushed his way through the crowd, asked him what he meant.

—This nutter thinks he's a tree, the finder explained. —We're sure of it — he really thinks he's a tree!

Suchandsuch nodded.

—All right. So if he thinks he's a tree, then he *is* a tree.

—What're we gonna do with him, Such? Put him on the fire?

—We could use some more firewood, agreed Suchandsuch. —Okay, put him on top of the pile. I just hope he burns real good, that's all.

The idea was greeted with yells of jolly sadism. Once again Ariston was seized and lifted, and he was being carried towards the bonfire when the cars with the girls and the bulk of the beer came honking onto the scene. The cars drew up and screeching, waving females, already half-drunk, tumbled and staggered out. All interest in Ariston evaporated. He was nonchalantly tossed to one side. He fell on top of a bike, his head hit the engine with a thud, and he blacked out.

When he came to it was dark. Out of the darkness came thudding music, shouts, yells, some of the voices, screeching and gibbering, not even sounding human. The party had been going for long enough to have progressed from merely feral to self-destructive. Ariston was glad to see the bonfire had been lit without him. It flared against the night, crackling and snapping, sending sparks whirling up into the sky. Silhouettes constantly weaved backwards and forwards in front of the flames. Someone tripped over Ariston, picked himself up and stumbled away mumbling curses. A fight broke out between two of the silhouettes and the air was filled with shouts and snarls. A figure was thrown into the bonfire, leapt out with a scream and ran shrieking down to the lake to dowse its blazing clothes and hair. It looked like being a swell party.

HIS JOINTS were stiff. His muscles ached. His head throbbed. He had fled from the Nihilists and escaped through the forest in the darkness. Soon after first light he had reached a cart-track and this had eventually brought him to a metaled road. Although it was now some time after dawn the air was bitterly cold. A gray mist hung over the long straight strip of macadam and made it seem to stretch from nothingness to nothingness. There was no sound of any kind. In spite of the cold and damp Ariston sat down on the grass verge. He was too tired to walk any farther. He was exhausted, hungry, lost. When a car or truck came along he would thumb a lift.

As the sun strengthened the mist cleared. While Ariston had been sitting there resting not one vehicle of any type had passed in either direction. He gazed hopelessly down the road. The morning wore on and there was still no traffic. He'd never get a lift. Not on this road. It was in good enough condition, to judge by the look of it – a fine, four-lane road with no grass or weeds growing on it, no holes – but obviously, for some reason, no longer in use. It didn't matter. He'd stay where he was, anyway. He'd have to. He didn't have the energy to go on. He needed something to eat. Something, anything. He remembered the birds, the glossy black birds with their yellow beaks. Some nuts and berries would have been very welcome right now. Anything would have been welcome. Food, food, food, the problem was always food.

He was lightheaded with hunger and exhaustion. His nerves were worn out. He kept imagining he heard a car approaching. Time after time he deluded himself with aural mirages. Time and again he lifted his drooping head from his knees and saw that there was no car and no truck, only an empty road. Finally he learned to ignore the sounds. The more realistic they were, the more he pretended not to hear. The road became quite busy with phantom vehicles. He refused to be gulled. Then there was a squeal of brakes, as if a car had drawn up. He paid no attention. A woman's voice spoke to him. Slowly he raised his head. Cars and trucks were zooming past in both directions and drawn up in front of him was a beautiful black limousine. The woman behind the wheel beckoned. Ariston hauled himself to his feet and grabbed the handle of the front passenger door. The driver smiled.

—I'm afraid that door's stuck, she said. —The lock's broken. Get in the back.

He pulled the rear door open, scrambled in and slammed the door shut. The car moved smoothly off. Ariston saw there was a glass partition separating the back of the interior from the front. When the young woman spoke again her words issued from an intercom speaker set below the partition. She told him to make himself comfortable. That was all she said. No questions about where he wanted to go. That suited him. He didn't know where he wanted to go. One place was a good as another. He glanced up and saw she was examining him in the rear-view mirror. She smiled at him again.

—Relax, she said.

He settled back in the seat. Genuine leather. Hey, this was a lucky break. Being driven about in a luxury car by a beautiful chauffeuse was all right. A car like this did things for you. If you had a car like this you were important. But he was still hungry. Even important people need food. There was a click, a hissing noise. He didn't notice. He was busy deciding what he would have for lunch. He was creating a superb menu, discussing it with the head waiter. The sauces, the wines ... The head waiter dared to contradict him on one choice, did he? No, no, not contradict – he had meant merely to suggest. He apologized if he had seemed to correct m'sieur. M'sieur was undoubtedly the finest judge of a balanced menu he had ever met, the most sophisticated of gourmets ...

The hissing continued. M'sieur was rather pale. Didn't he feel well? No, he did not feel well. He felt as though his head was floating away from his body. M'sieur was losing consciousness, it seemed. M'sieur was slipping, sliding, slowly toppling sideways. ...

Now m'sieur was slumped unconscious across the genuine leather seat.

The driver, watching in the rear-view mirror smiled and flicked a switch on the dashboard. The hissing stopped. The car continued to hurl forward.

VALERY CLIMBED the dusty rubbish-strewn stairs of the condemned and deserted building. Some of the apartment doors were boarded up; others had been kicked in by exploring kids, and the dead hallways and rooms with their oddments of dilapidated furniture lay exposed. The gaping doorways had a pathetic air of abandonment that beseeched a little human interest. These places had once been homes. But Valery had made this trip too often to have any curiosity, and she passed upwards without a single sideways glance.

When she reached the top floor she went to one of the doors and took a keyring from her handbag. She unlocked the door, went into the apartment, closed the door behind her. Her footsteps resounded from the bare floorboards as she stepped briskly along the narrow corridor. She stopped outside the end door, and after she'd checked her appearance in her compact mirror and tugged down the jacket of her elegant two-piece suit she entered the room.

It was a room as dusty and forsaken as all the others in the building. There was no furniture or furnishing except for a torn mattress in one corner. On the mattress lay Ariston. He was chained to the wall by his left ankle.

Valery smiled brightly.

—Guess who, Ariston!

He didn't look up or give any sign acknowledging her arrival. He had become terribly thin, little more than a skeleton, and the skin stretched tightly over his bones had an unhealthy yellowish hue. She crossed the room towards him. Her face wore an exaggerated expression of concern.

—What's the matter? Why don't you answer?

She bent over him and reached out as though to touch his cheek, but her fingers remained poised a fraction away from the stubbled skin.

—What's the matter? she cooed. —Aren't you well? Is my little Ariston feeling badly – or is he just sulking again?

She gave his shoulder a playful push. He was so weak it was enough to topple him over. He lay motionless, sprawled on his side with one arm folded awkwardly under him. Still he hadn't looked at her.

Valery turned away and went to stand by the window with her back to him. Her face bulged with suppressed smiles and laughter.

—It's a fine day today, she remarked when she had gained control of herself. —Shall I open the window and let in some fresh air? It would do you good. Really, you should get out more.

Again, wheezing with amusement, shaking her head from side to side, her eyes squeezed shut, she struggled with her delighted appreciation of her humor.

—No, really, Ariston, she went on when she had recovered, you don't realize how stuffy it is in here.

She took hold of the window and pretended to try to raise it. After a few fake attempts she stopped.

—Seems to be stuck, she chuckled. —Just like the car door – eh, Ariston?

Ariston stirred.

—Why do we have to go through this every time? he murmured.

His ghost of a voice seemed to come from far away. Valery put her hand to her ear.

—What, did you say something? Through *what* every time? Through *what*?

He didn't answer. She approached him slowly.

—Through what? she repeated softly. —Through what?

Moisture appeared in his eyes, gathered into drops and trickled down his cheeks. Valery observed this exhibition of emotion with a show of interest and tenderness.

—I love you when you cry, Ariston. You look quite beautiful when you're like that.

He moaned almost inaudibly.

—I do love you, Ariston. Don't ever doubt it. Look, I'll tell you what. …

She dipped into her handbag and fetched out the bunch of keys, then knelt and undid the padlock that fastened his chain to the wall.

—I've set you free, Ariston. Now what do you say for that?

—Thank you, he breathed.

—That's right, she nodded, returning the keys to her bag and bringing out something else, which she held behind her back. —And I've got a present for you. Guess what?

—I don't know, he sighed.

—Guess!

—Please. Don't torture me.

She lifted her eyebrows.

—Torture? Why use such a word? I'm only asking you to make a guess. C'mon, you must try. What would you like, for example?

—Food, he whispered.

—There you are, you're right! That was easy, wasn't it? But what kind of food?

—Give it to me. Please. …

—Give you what? You must say what it is you want.

—Food.

—But what kind?

—I don't know. …

—You don't know! Well, you can't be very hungry then, can you?

She waited, but he said nothing. He was less than half-conscious. Valery suddenly lost patience. She turned on her heel, throwing down the present as she did so. It was a crust of bread.

—There, she snapped. —Take it. It's yours. You're no fun to play with – you're just hopeless!

Ariston's eyes flickered. He focused on the crust. It had fallen quite near him. He could reach it. He shifted and stretched out a hand. He couldn't hold his arm steady. It swayed in the air like an antenna, an antenna that felt its way forward delicately, wavered, then collapsed. From a great distance came his whisper.

—Please. ... I can't reach it.

Valery, looking out of the window, didn't bother to glance round.

—Of course you can reach it, she said.

—I can't. ...

—Don't be silly. Go on, try again.

The antenna rose an inch from the floor, then collapsed once more. Ariston closed his eyes to shut out the terrible sight of the bread lying there, within reach, unreachable. He was barely conscious now. He thought Valery called his name several times but he wasn't sure. Then he felt vibrations as she walked away into one of the other rooms. She came back.

—Here you are, Ariston, she said gently. —Drink this.

He felt glass cool against his lips. His mouth filled with water. He swallowed.

—Better? she asked when he'd emptied the glass. —All right. Now pick up the bread and eat it.

He stirred. Slowly, painfully, he began to change his position. With a great effort he got up on his knees. He leaned towards the bread. Valery was standing beside it. As his hand was about to close on it she neatly flicked it away with the toe of her highly polished shoe.

—Same old game, he mumbled.

She laughed.

—Yes, the same old game.

—Why do we have to ...

—Don't talk so much. You'll waste your strength. Get the bread.

The crust was about three feet away. He began to crawl towards it, his chain rattling as he dragged it with him across the floor. Just as he reached the crust she knocked it away again. In this fashion they proceeded around the room. When they had come back to their original position Valery picked up the bread and put it in her handbag.

—There now, don't start crying again, she consoled. —You wouldn't really want to eat it – it's all dirty and horrible!

Then she fastened his chain to the wall.

Ariston sank onto the mattress. He wanted only to be left alone, but he knew she wouldn't go. Not yet. The next phase of the game was about to begin. She had taken up her position by the window and was whistling tunelessly to herself. When she spoke her voice was wispy with emotion.

—D'you know where I was this afternoon? she asked

—Where?

—In the park, she said, heaving a sigh. —Where we first met. Remember it?

—Yes, of course. I remember it as if … as if it was yesterday.

There was a pause.

—Well? she asked irritably. —Don't tell me you've forgotten what comes next?

—I'm sorry. ...

—"What were you doing there?" That's what's next, idiot.

—What were you doing there? he echoed dully.

—Oh nothing, just thinking, she said, her voice once again soft with nostalgia. —I felt I had to go there. I sat on the very same bench we used to sit on. You know the one. ...

—The one by the pond.

—How little you remember, she scolded with sickly sweetness. —Just like a man. No, it's the bench near the bandstand. I sat there and thought how wonderful it was for us once. We used to hold hands.

—Yes.

—So innocent. Like children.

—Yes.

—And the band used to play. ...

She began to waltz around the room, humming to herself. When she stopped dancing she stood in the middle of the room lost in reverie. After a few minutes she realized where she was. She turned to Ariston.

—It's no use – you're not playing you part with conviction. You never do. And you forgot your lines.

—I'm sorry.

—*I'm sorry*, she mimicked. —You stupid animal, you've annoyed me again, and I'd hoped you were going to do better today. I was going to be so nice to you. Now I've no choice but to punish you.

He was too weak to plead. Besides, he knew it was pointless. Valery left the room and returned almost immediately. In her hand was a short whip. She bent and pulled down his ragged jeans, revealing the sullen purple marks of other beatings.

—Well, Ariston, she mused, smiling, this is going to hurt you a lot more than it'll hurt me. ...

She smiled mirthlessly at her little worn-out joke, suddenly raised her arm and lashed the whip furiously down across his buttocks. Ariston cried out. His body tightened in a spasm of pain, jerking up off the mattress. Valery lifted a foot and kicked him flat onto his stomach. Again the whip rose in the air and came whistling down. The leather seared his flesh, cutting into old bruises. Again, again, again. ...

Then it was over. Legs straddling, slightly out of breath, Valery stood gazing down at her victim. Her cheeks were flushed with excitement and her long dark hair fell in loosened strands over her face. She had never looked more beautiful. Ariston lay moaning on the filthy mattress, and slowly the harsh triumph melted from Valery's face. Her eyes moistened. She threw the whip away from her and knelt beside him, tenderly running the tips of her fingers over the fresh weals.

—Oh, look what I've done to your little behind! she sobbed. —So sorry, I'm so sorry, Ariston – I didn't really want to! Let me make it better. ...

For a while, cooing maternally, she kissed and stroked his buttocks. Later, when Ariston's moans had died away, she pulled up his jeans, patted him on the backside, picked up the whip and went out.

Some minutes passed.

When she reappeared her hair had been tidied and her make-up freshened.

—I've got to go now, she said brightly. —Busy-busy, you know. I'll see you sometime.

She paused at the door and stared at him. Without another word she tossed him the crust of bread, then left.

THE ROOM swayed. The walls undulated. The light from the window hurt his eyes. He was aware that he was no longer alone. She had returned. He heard her voice, felt the blows, but paid neither much attention. The voice faded away to silence, the light to darkness. The room disappeared. Then there was moisture on his lips. His parched tongue licked at it. The room manifested itself. Water filled his mouth, too much water. It was difficult to swallow. His throat was blocked with water but still it came, more water. He couldn't breathe, he was drowning. He coughed out the water and immediately felt a blow across his face.

Men. They took advantage of a girl because she was open-hearted. Had their fun and left you. But not now. She'd learned. She knew how to treat them now. She'd teach this one something about pain, give him a taste of what she'd gone through. The birth had nearly killed her, the bleeding afterwards nearly drained her. And the kid, it was a good thing it had died. It would've been a monster – it *was* a monster. Even the doctor turned his face away. That's why he let it die. He didn't try to invigorate it, just laid it aside. Later it'd been put in a plastic bag and taken to some laboratory. An interesting specimen. Photographed, measured, dissected, discussed, finally incinerated. Up in smoke, that's where it went. The fruit of her womb. Up the chimney. That's romance for you. The man goes off laughing, the woman suffers. The man adds your name to his list of conquests, boasts how many women he's had. The woman gets herself split in two. That's love for you. Up the chimney it goes, the man goes on his merry way. That was how it was. The man just laughed and went on his way. He didn't know about what happened and didn't care. They take their fun and forget you. But she hadn't forgotten. Now she knew how to treat them. She'd learned the hard way. It had been lovely at first. He was nice. But no, he wasn't, he was really a monster – that's why the kid was a monster too. He should've gone up the chimney with his kid. He should've burned – so BURN NOW!

She stabbed her cigarette into Ariston's face, grinding it out in the flesh under his right eye. He screamed and shuddered back into his corner, his skinny legs drawn up, arms shielding his face. Valery, hunched over him, shivered with delight, gloated. Then, straightening up, she closed her eyes, her face changed, like the face of someone falling asleep. She stood perfectly still as the seconds passed.

When she opened her eyes her face was calm. She smiled serenely at Ariston and leaned over him again, gently drawing his arms away from his face.

—Have I hurt you, Ariston? Let's have a peek. Ah, dear me, that doesn't look so good, that nasty mark, does it? Well, we'll see if there isn't something we can do to cover it up. ...

She patted his cheek and left the room, returning a few moments later carrying a blue vanity case.

—Actually, Ariston, I had something like this in mind for you anyway. A little surprise. I thought it would be a nice new game for us.

She knelt beside him and quickly stripped off his rags. Ariston, pulled and pushed one way and another by her brisk hands, could offer no resistance. When he was completely naked Valery opened the vanity case and took out a pink brassiere.

—Like it? she asked, dangling it in front of him. —I bought it specially for you. Took a long time choosing it, so don't try to tell me it doesn't suit you because I know it does.

She shoved his arms through the straps and hooked up the back. The bra hung loosely across his chest. Valery smiled mockingly as she propped him up into a sitting position against the cracked wall.

She set to work on his face. Every other day or so she had shaved him to remove, or at least reduce, the detested growth of beard, that sign of his maleness. Now, once again, she ran the electric shaver harshly over his stubbly cheeks. That done, she briskly spread foundation cream over his cheeks, then powdered them a chalky white. At his cheekbones she rouged two neat gaudy circles. Next the lips were colored a bright red, so that a wide vulgarly sensual mouth covered Ariston's own. He was conscious enough to know what she was doing. He didn't care. All he cared about was that she wouldn't hurt him any more. At the moment she wasn't hurting him, and for that he was grateful. His head felt unbearably heavy, but he tried to keep it steady for her.

Valery had started on his eyes. Green eye-shadow had been brushed on and now, frowning with concentration, she was drawing a black eyeliner along one upper lid. She was enjoying herself. Give him that really tarty look. Make a real whore out of him the way men had tried to make a whore out of her. She paused as she finished one eye, peered critically at her handiwork, then licked the eyeliner and turned her attention to the other eye.

—Right, then, she announced, putting away the cosmetics. —Just one more thing and there we are, pretty as a picture.

From the case beside her she produced a pair of ridiculously long false eyelashes. Carefully she fixed them on.

—Now take a look at yourself, dearie, she said, holding up a mirror. —Go on, take a look at what an attractive girl you are.

Ariston blinked his eyes open. He saw a bewildered stranger staring back at him. A crazed clown's face. A caricature.

—And of course we mustn't forget a woman's crowning glory, must we?

And she lifted up a curly blonde wig.

Her strong hands seized his head and fitted the wig firmly with quick adept tugs. That done to her satisfaction, she held the mirror in front of him again for a few seconds to let him appreciate the full effect. Then, reaching out and taking hold of Ariston under the shoulders, she stood up, hauling him to his feet with her. His knees buckled as his legs failed under his weight and, as he started to slide down, she had to grab him and lean him up against the wall.

—Stop pretending to be so weak, Ariston, she scolded. —After all, I fed you the day before yesterday – or did I forget again? Oh, what am I *like*?

Her laugh cracked the dead stillness of the ruined apartment. Then she was suddenly serious. She eyed the bra and shook her head doubtfully.

—That just won't do, she murmured, grabbing the bra and jerking it up and down scornfully. —Most unpersuasive. You're flat, Ariston dearie. A real flatty. Wait a minute, though. ...

Valery unfastened the bra and tossed it away. She swooped and picked the lipstick up out of the vanity case, straightening up just in time to steady her tottering captive. Holding the emaciated body up against the wall with one hand, she used the lipstick to paint a circle round the left nipple. Another circle was drawn around the right nipple and the nipples themselves smeared with the red grease.

—That's better, she said, standing back and viewing him.

Unsupported, Ariston swayed but managed not to collapse. Valery's fever-bright eyes flicked critically up and down him. She nodded.

—Now for the very last thing, she said, grabbing his prick. —We'll have to do something about *this*, won't we? It doesn't quite go with your lovely new tits.

Again her hand dipped into the vanity case. It reappeared clutching a large pair of scissors which she flourished under his nose, snapping them open and shut, while her other hand jerked viciously at his prick.

—I really think you'd be better off without that thing down there, Ariston. I mean, it really must be terribly awkward having something like that hanging between your legs. ...

She giggled and placed his prick between the half-open blades.

—It must get in your way. I'm sure it must. Now let's see, where shall we cut? ...

Slowly she measured down from the tip.

—Here? she suggested, closing the blades slightly so that they nicked the skin.

Blood oozed out. Ariston whimpered.

—No, down a bit more. ... Here, maybe?

Blood trickled along the gleaming steel. Ariston was trembling. One hand pawed her in shaky protest. She brushed it aside.

—No, farther down still, I think, she said, moving the scissors. —Right down. *Right at the root, eh?*

Ariston's painted mouth opened and a gasp of despair, a sound coming from beyond pain, escaped. Blood ran down his thighs and dripped to the dirty floorboards. Valery gazed down at the spattering drops of crimson, then looked up into Ariston's dull, out-of-focus eyes.

—But Ariston, she whispered in mock sympathy, why didn't you tell me it was your time of the month?

She laughed, laughed, laughed, laughed. *His time of the month.* Oh, that was a good one. It was too, too funny. Couldn't be funnier. The air vibrated with wild laughter. The window rattled in a gale of insane mirth. The walls of the room threw her shrieks back into Ariston's face and her own. The room itself became a great gaping mouth laughing, mocking them both, the evil joke that was their lives.

—A gruesome twosome, that's us. Eh, Ariston? We've got togetherness. *Love*, did you say? Was that the word? *Love*?

Valery thought her sides would split. Tears rolled down her cheeks. But Ariston didn't seem to see the joke at all. Why not? Had he no sense of humor? Valery prodded him with the scissors. That would help him to *get the point*. The blades pierced his navel. That would liven him up a little.

She laughed on and on and jabbed him again, again, punctuating her laughter by puncturing him. But she was laughing so much that she couldn't put any real force into it. The scissors weren't going in very far. Hardly at all, really. Hardly any blood. She gave him another dig in the belly, for he still didn't see the joke. She poked at his ribs, aimed at his painted nipples, jabbed and jabbed at her targets until his chest streamed with blood.

Ariston staggered and reeled, his chain rattling. Laughing, laughing – because he was such a funny sight, and it was all such a funny joke, all of it, everything, him, his life, her life, everyone's life, it all really was – laughing, she aimed higher, jabbed at his throat, his whore's mouth. His upper lip split and spurted blood. One stabbed cheek bled over its rouge, red rivaling red.

But his eyes. That's it. *His eyes. Go for his eyes.* ...

Suddenly a voice, thin, high, but loaded with outrage, rang out:

—LEAVE HIM ALONE!

As though struck by a powerful sideswiping blow, Valery spun round, staggered, the scissors dropping with a clatter.

In the doorway stood Jacksall. In his hand was a gun and it was pointing straight at her. Stunned, wordless, she stared at him.

—Don't you lay another finger on him, Jacksall commanded, his voice trembling with outrage. —I own sixty per cent of that boy and I want it in working condition. Now you just move yourself over there.

He waved the gun in the direction of the wall opposite the window. Valery appeared not to understand, as though he had spoken in a foreign language, just made noises.

—DO IT! Jacksall screamed at her.

Slowly, like someone awakening, she obeyed.

Jacksall hurried across to Ariston, who had subsided onto the mattress, started to try to help him to his feet, then saw the chain and padlock.

—The key, he said to Valery, snapping his fingers. —Where is it?

She didn't answer.

—The KEY! he screamed again.

—In my handbag, she muttered.

His eyes followed the direction of her glance to where the handbag was lying on the floor. He nodded at it.

—All right, give it to me.

She didn't move, just stared at him. He raised the gun higher, aiming it at her head.

—Die in a few minutes or die now. Make your choice.

She stood looking at him blankly, without concern, for a couple of seconds, then stepped over to the handbag, picked it up and moved slowly towards him. The arm holding the bag began to rise, as though she was about to pass the bag to Jacksall, and Jacksall started to reach out to take it. Instead, in a flash, before he knew what was happening, she had swung her arm in a curve, released the bag, knocked the gun out of his grip. The gun thudded onto the floorboards. Both rushed for it. They grappled.

Jacksall found her surprisingly strong. They rolled backwards and forwards on the floor. She clawed his face, he punched hers. The fight escalated, as fights will. They kneed each other in the belly. She drove a thumb into one of his eyes and gouged it out. He grabbed her arm, twisted it ferociously and there was the snap of breaking bone. Neither screamed. The only sound from their mouths was the rasp of their breathing. It was as though they felt no pain.

The injuries they inflicted became even more terrible. They were two gladiators in the arena. Each had ripped the other's clothes to rags; now they began to tear at the flesh itself. The floor became covered in blood, the walls were spattered and smeared with it.

Lying in the room of blood, Ariston saw, quite near him, Valery's handbag. He reached for it, stretched. He had it. He clutched it, pulled it closer, opened it and fumbled inside for the bunch of keys. Holding the padlock in one shaking hand, he tried one key, failed, struggled with another. None of the keys would fit. The last one. Yes. Yes, it fitted in, started to turn. But then it stuck. It wasn't the key's fault, it was the padlock. It was being difficult, opposing him out of sheer spite. Then it had a sudden change of mind, took pity on him, sprung open. He was free.

He began to crawl towards the door. Jacksall and Valery tripped over him without noticing what it was they'd tripped over. They were as absorbed in each other as two lovers. It was a fight to the loving, passionate death. Scraps of skin and flesh littered the floor. A hank of hair. Jacksall's gouged eyeball ogled Ariston as he crept by. A torn-off finger pointed to the exit. He followed its directions, dragged himself out through the doorway. His blood-wet hands and knees stuck with dust, he crawled, tumbled, rolled down the dirty stairs.

Still on hands and knees, he emerged into the empty street, dragged himself along the pavement, turned to the right, dragged himself along, turned to the left, went on, on ...

He found himself by the river. Tall weeds grew there, rank and sickly smelling. He pushed his way through them to the water's edge. A little boat, gaily painted, was waiting to take him away. It invited him aboard. He fell in. The boat rocked, loosed itself from the mud. Slowly it moved into the current. Ariston, lying in state, was carried downstream.

The river wound down through the city. It was dusk, and the city lights flaunted themselves in all their vulgarity against the oncoming darkness. Ariston passed the movie studios, the candy factories, the fairgrounds. Lights blazed all around, glittering the surface of the water. Distant music blared.

Ariston passed on. The unmistakable effluvia of the rubbish dump came to his nostrils. His old home. He tried to raise himself up to see if his shack was still there. He caught a glimpse of it. Its door opened and someone came out. At first he couldn't make out who it was. Then he saw it was Malk. And he was waving. He was calling to Ariston but the words were unintelligible. On top of a rubbish tip that sloped down to the water stood Bobs, Sonny and Toots. They too waved, they played and sang. Some fans were there too. Doll people lined the river's banks like artificial flowers. Even Pete was there, lying in his coffin.

Ariston sank back into the boat. He resigned himself to the river, this river of forever that, smooth and gentle as the approach of sleep, was floating him past his past. As it flowed down its banks spread farther apart, spreading farther and farther apart until they were so distant they were mere lines, thin and vague. Then, as the boat drifted into the estuary, the lines were erased. He could smell the sea.

Except as an angry glow against the ever-darkening sky, the city had disappeared, and even the glow was fading ... fading away behind ... fading ... Gone. Nothing. He would never see the city again. He had escaped.

Adrift on the open sea. Now it was completely dark. He was alone, completely and at last alone. It was very peaceful. He lay at ease in the little boat as in a bed, his own little first and last bed, at ease and at peace.

Peace. At long last, peace was his.

Here river merges with sea, and here no horizon line defines water and sky. Here all that seemed ours, all we assumed made us who we were, is stripped away, the I, that gabbling fool, silenced, as finite enters infinity and is totally consumed.

Floating on the River of Forever

Printed in Great Britain
by Amazon

56978286R00079